Praise for

Darcy Maguire spends her days as a matchmaker, torturing tall, handsome men, seducing them into believing in love, and romancing their socks off! And when she's not working on her novels, she enjoys gardening, reading and going to the movies. She loves to hear from readers. Visit her at www.darcymaguire.com

Recent titles by the same author:

THE FIANCÉE CHARADE
A CONVENIENT GROOM*
THE BEST MAN'S BABY*
A PROFESSIONAL ENGAGEMENT*
ALMOST MARRIED

The Bridal Business trilogy

THE BRIDAL CHASE

BY
DARCY MAGUIRE

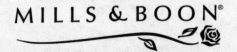

MILLS & BOON®

MILLS & BOON and MILLS & BOON with the Rose Device are registered trademarks of the publisher.

First published in Great Britain 2005
Harlequin Mills & Boon Limited,
Eton House, 18-24 Paradise Road, Richmond, Surrey TW9 1SR

© Debra D'Arcy 2005

ISBN 0 263 84245 2

Set in Times Roman 10½ on 13 pt.
02-0705-37628

Printed and bound in Spain
by Litografía Rosés, S.A., Barcelona

CHAPTER ONE

ROXANNE GRAY glanced up at the ceiling dragging in a ragged breath. The bar was crass, loud *and* a cliché, but it had to be at *his* local.

She figured she had to seem available and willing to roll between the covers with him with only the smallest effort on his part.

Oh, gawd. *What had she got herself into?*

It had taken her for ever to work out that she couldn't just go anywhere to pick him up. It couldn't be at a library or he'd think she was too smart to fall straight into bed with him. And it couldn't be at a shopping mall because, goodness, although she'd be awfully comfortable and at home, she couldn't wait that long until he went into one.

Roxanne toyed with the stem of her glass to still her shaking hands. It couldn't be on public transport because he probably didn't take it—he was the sort of guy who would have a really nice car parked somewhere…and if by chance he did take the bus or train, what was the likelihood he'd consider a woman who made eye contact? Even if it was just for sex?

She glanced around the room, taking a deep breath to calm herself, pushing the thought far from her mind. Just meeting him was all she had to worry about, for now.

His workplace had seemed a nice safe environment for her to engineer a meeting with him, but there were just too many rules for office decorum and propriety to wade through before she'd have been able to get what she needed.

She glanced towards the door, the thought of escape on her mind. She didn't have to step this far out of her comfort zone to prove anything...*or did she?*

Roxanne shook herself. This had to be done. She needed a quick, efficient approach and this was it. The only logical option left to her was a club like this.

She had to smile at the cliché *she* made, sitting at a bar in a short black dress with a plunging neckline. She clutched her strawberry daiquiri as if it was a lifeline to sanity.

She couldn't believe she was doing this...

Roxanne stroked the book beside her, struggling with her rising panic. It had given her a few ideas on how to do this. She'd picked it up from a little book-shop down the street. It dedicated an entire chapter to the arts of picking up a woman...she couldn't find one on how to pick up a guy. Either it wasn't that hard or women didn't usually do it. Either way, she figured the book had at least given her a few hints.

She took another gulp of her daiquiri, savouring the fruity sweetness, praying the double jigger of rum she'd asked for had given her the courage to go through with this.

Gawd, she hoped he liked her and fell into her trap—hook, line and sinker.

Roxanne tried to smile at the barman, but failed. The mass of pick-up lines swirled in her head, the litany of conversation starters, and the burden of the result she was looking for was all she could cope with.

She swung around on her stool, trying to ignore the cold knot forming in her belly. The bar was filling fast with suits from all quarters of the city sector stopping in for a quick drink before the long haul homeward, most probably to partners and kids. Some just meeting up with others to take the trip with, or to join friends to go out somewhere else.

The bar was a trendy place deep in Sydney's business sector, with just the right balance of class and approachability. The artworks on the walls were modern, the solid colours lit by bright lights shining only on them, the rest of the room bathed in the shadows and the reflected light, giving a mood of intimacy and privacy despite the lack of space.

The black faux-marble bar stretched almost across the room, with matching tables with their own chrome bar stools perched beside them, placed to maximize the capacity rather than for comfort zones. And Roxanne was as far from her comfort zone as she could get.

She didn't want to be here, *or* meet *him*.

Cade Taylor Watson…what a name. She glanced at the photo of him that she was using as a bookmark. His large square jaw, his strong brow, his chiselled features giving his image a strength and a presence that she could feel right down to her toes.

Her hand still shook as she lifted her glass again. This wasn't going to be easy.

She took a big gulp of her drink, scanning the room again, half-afraid she'd missed him, yet more terrified that she hadn't.

He stood by the door.

Her heart slammed into her chest.

He was easy to spot. He stood a good six inches taller than the suits around him. His finely tailored suit was deep blue. His hair was cut short at the sides, the longer top slightly spiked, the colour an almost rusty-blond that seemed to match his eyes—a golden hazel, and his gaze careered around the room.

His attention rested on her only a moment and kept moving, obviously looking for someone…else.

She let out the breath she was holding, the pressure in her chest easing. O-kay. So he hadn't been magnetically drawn to her the way she'd sort of hoped he would. She would have preferred it if he'd locked eyes with hers, his feet moving him closer, and she would have dazzled him with her pick-up lines and conversation starters.

Dammit. Now she had to go and break the ice herself.

She gulped some more of the Dutch courage in her glass. Could she just sit on this stool and hope she radiated enough charm and allure that he'd buy her a drink? Could she afford to wait, to rely on her looks and short black dress to get her the result she needed?

No.

She jerked to her feet, slowly smoothed down the fabric of her dress on the off chance he was watching, picked up her handbag and sauntered over to the guy.

Her blood rushed hot and fiery to her cheeks.

She walked slowly, conscious of the thrust of her breasts, of the sway of her hips, of the distance that was vanishing between her and where he sat on his stool at a small table near the window.

This was it. She could do this. She was a professional…or temping as one, and that was as good as being one, wasn't it?

He was hunched over the small table, a pen in his hand, scribbling on a napkin. His shopping list? His workload? A dear Jane letter?

She tapped him on his large square shoulder, acutely aware of the warmth under her fingertip, of the man beneath the suit and just how long it had been since she'd been this close to one, let alone touched one.

Roxanne swallowed hard. 'Excuse me,' she said softly. Darn it, a woman on the prowl didn't have confidence issues. She should be strong, independent and daring.

He turned towards her, the pen in his hand. 'Yes?'

His deep rich voice washed over her, seeping into her skin and making every nerve stand on alert.

She opened her mouth but the words wouldn't come—Cade Taylor Watson...was a hunk!

His warm gaze met hers and careered over her in quick assessment, taking in her attire, and hopefully the shape of her body that she'd slithered into the dress.

Was he thinking how nicely they'd fit together? How her hands would feel running over that incredibly fine body of his, of her lips tracing the muscles on his wide chest, of her curling her fingers in his light hair, or of them fusing together?

Roxanne opened her mouth, and closed it. So, he was more handsome than she could have imagined...there was an energy about him that wasn't captured in the photo, that one could only feel in the flesh, first hand. And dammit she was feeling it.

'Can I help you?' he offered, his golden-flecked eyes warm and inviting.

She licked her lips, the welcoming flicker she saw boosting her will. 'I—' Oh, help. Weather? Politics? A straight-out invitation to get down and dirty with her?

He raised an eyebrow, rotating the pen in his right hand like a mini baton. 'I...' She pulled her attention from the sexy shape of his lips to meet his eyes. She could do this. She'd researched, practised and was primed. She clenched her hands by her sides. 'Are your legs tired?' She tried to smile like the book said. 'Because you've been running through my dreams.'

'Wow,' he murmured, a smile fighting his sensuous mouth. 'I don't think I've heard that one before.'

'Ever used it?' she said in a rush.

'No, but I have used a few others in my time.'

She couldn't help but smile. This wasn't so bad. He wasn't going to jump on her or anything…pity. It would have made this so much easier. 'I probably should have gone with something about the weather…' she offered tentatively.

He rubbed his jaw as though trying to smother his smile. 'Wouldn't have been as memorable or as cute.'

She clasped her hands gently in front of her, holding them tightly, a bubble of excitement rising up inside. They were talking, clicking. This was going to be no problem at all. 'Thanks, you wouldn't believe how hard this is.'

Cade nodded, raising an eyebrow, putting the pen in his shirt pocket along with the napkin. 'I know. I've done it enough times myself but I have to say it's not often I get the opportunity of being on the receiving end.'

'Really? I would think that women everywhere would take a punt and chat you up.' Was she smiling too much? She could feel her cheeks aching…she was. She tried to sober under his warm gaze.

'You're the first.'

'So—' She glanced wildly around the room. This was it. Phase two. She'd got his attention, now all she had to do was get a sign he wanted to do more than chat to her. 'Can I—'

Someone tapped her on the shoulder. She turned, pulling her gaze away from Cade's, forcing herself to focus on the interruption rather than the gorgeous challenge at hand.

'You left your book, Miss,' the barman said, thrusting something towards her. 'On the bar.'

Oh, no. She yanked the book out of the guy's hands where he was brandishing it around for everyone to see, including Cade. *How to be a Stud* was not going to help her cause at all.

She stuffed the book into her handbag, fighting with the corners to get the zip up, the seconds melting into a minute that felt too long.

Roxanne swung around to face her mark, forcing a smile on her face.

His seat was empty.

A sense of loss filled her. She tried to laugh at her defeat, but couldn't. What had happened?

Had he gone to get her a drink, gone to the bathroom, or to talk to a friend? Roxanne scanned the room but there weren't any tall rusty-blond hunks to be seen.

She'd lost him.

What was her sister going to say when she heard

about this? She was meant to be helping her, not making a mess of things.

A glimpse of a blue suit caught her eye through the sign on the front window. Cade Taylor Watson was on the footpath outside, his arm around a woman.

She moved closer to the window.

Roxanne recognised her instantly, the sight a steel weight in the pit of her belly, reminding her of her decision to do this, of her sister and of her miserable failure.

She sagged against the windowsill. She'd mucked it up. Her first attempt at being a private investigator-cum-seductress and she'd failed, miserably, but then she hadn't had long.

He'd been late.

She was early.

And she was left with nothing.

CHAPTER TWO

CADE glanced back towards the bar, a dull ache sliding into his chest.

Given different circumstances, like a few months earlier, and it would have taken a hurricane to tear him away from a unique and tantalising woman like her. Now all it took was Heather.

He'd had no other choice. Heather had arrived right on time. He'd wanted to say goodbye to the tall, curvaceous beauty with the pick-up line and amazing smile, but it was wise not to have. Heather would not have understood.

Heather may be beautiful, successful and classy, but tolerant she was not. Meeting her at a gallery opening just after deciding it was time to settle down and get married had seemed like fate. She'd seemed perfect.

He steered Heather towards the car park, focusing on the footpath and his fiancée beside him and not the woman he'd just left.

He should have said something to her. It didn't have to be a lot. Just to let her know that he appreciated her wit, her attention and her smile. The thought of putting her off being so confident and charming…

The guilt sat heavy in his gut.

He swung to Heather. 'So how was your day?' he blurted, opening the door on his black Lexus.

'Oh, just the usual, honey. What about yours?' she lilted, shooting him one of her dazzling smiles.

'Fine.'

She swung and faced him, stabbing him with a piercing gaze, her eyes glittering dangerously. 'Did I see you talking to a pretty woman back there?'

The question was loaded, like a double-barrelled shotgun aimed at his chest. He knew she'd already come to her own conclusion, her tone said it all.

He shrugged as innocently as he could manage. Damage control was all he could offer. 'The one that wanted to know the time?' he offered diplomatically, striding around the car.

The woman had wanted to pick him up but Heather didn't have to know that. It would just upset her, and there was no way in the world he wanted to do that. Besides, nothing had happened.

'So where are we going tonight?' she said more cheerily as though she'd already dropped the matter.

He was thankful. He didn't want to go there… He wasn't sure he should be feeling like this, about anyone except Heather.

He just didn't seem as close to his fiancée as he first had been. There was no doubt that she had heaps to do, what with her busy career, her obligations to family and friends and planning their wedding.

The wedding seemed to take all the spare time she

had, despite having a wedding planner and both his and her mothers' help. But then the wedding was only two weeks away now.

He took a deep breath. It would all be fine after the wedding. Like it used to be. Besides, everyone loved her. *He loved her.* There wasn't anything more to it.

Cade just wished their approaching nuptials didn't occupy all her time. He'd wanted to spend a lot of time with her, get to know her even more.

He sighed. He guessed they had the rest of their lives for that.

'Does dinner at The Palace sound okay to you?' he asked, slipping behind the wheel.

Heather liked to be wined and dined at the finest of places and surprised with treats and gifts, and he loved seeing her happy. Which reminded him. He reached into the back seat and pulled out a small wrapped package. 'For you.'

'Oh, thank you,' she lilted, fluttering her eyelashes at him as he started the car. 'You know I love surprises, darling.'

He nodded, starting the car, quelling the image of being with that tall, mysterious beauty. He had everything and there was no way he'd risk that for anything.

He glanced at the woman who would soon be his wife, the tension easing from his shoulders. She was impeccably dressed, as she always was. Groomed and preened to perfection; even after a day's work at the fashion house that she managed she looked like a million dollars. Not the same sort of perfection as the stranger in the bar...hers was more a natural beauty, something she had without effort.

He could almost smell the stranger's sweet vanilla scent on the edge of his memory.

He caught himself. It didn't matter. Heather loved her top-shelf perfume, her designer wardrobe, his family and *him*...that was all that mattered.

They were going to have the perfect life together. She was everything he'd always wanted.

Roxanne dropped her head on to the desk, lifting and dropping it again for good measure. Why?

What was wrong with her?

Why had she even tried to pick the guy up with only minutes before his fiancée turned up? As if he was going to do anything then anyway...he wouldn't have even been considering her. There would be no way even the most daring man would risk it.

She couldn't stop thinking about it.

She rubbed the sore spot on her forehead. Maybe his impending date wouldn't have mattered to him if her dress had been shorter, sexier, red?

She sighed, dropping her head again on to the desk and staying there, covering her face. She was hopeless.

What sort of professional was she? She hadn't even looked at her watch to check out how much time she had...hadn't even thought about it after he had walked in that door, towering above the mortals, looking like a god in that tailored suit.

She would have thought it would have been easier, especially after all those detective novels she'd read and the shows she'd watched on TV.

She stared around the small office in the two-storey walk-up that her sister, Nadine, had found to run her business. It wasn't exactly typical of an investigator's office.

It was small, the size of a small apartment, with enough room for two desks, a couple of wastepaper baskets and three walls of filing cabinets that Nadine's daughter, Rory, had decorated with crayon.

A small pile of toys sat in the corner on a miniature desk where Rory came to help out when pre-school was out and the holidays were on.

One window looked out on the neighbouring office block's western wall and had floral curtains and the other faced the street with pink blinds that wouldn't go down.

The outer office was painted a soft peach with the paint that her sister had left over from painting her daughter's bedroom, with a sofa that had seen better days and a pile of magazines from the Dark Ages.

Despite appearances, Nadine said the business was going quite well…if you didn't count today's disaster or the fact that Roxanne had been left to hold the fort—and she had no experience in this type of fort at all.

What she was going to do now with the Cade case she had no idea. Half of her wanted to shove the thing into the filing cabinet and forget about it, the other half hankered to go and see the guy again, to try again.

Could she?

No. It would be too obvious and far too awkward for her, and the fact that her track record with men was a disaster had to be taken into account.

The door burst open.

Nadine rushed into the room, carrying an armload of files. 'What are you still doing here?' She glanced at her watch. 'It's late.'

Roxanne looked at the clock on the wall. 'Yes.' But she hadn't wanted to go home and face her sister until she'd worked out what to do.

'Don't think you can weasel overtime out of me.' Her sister shot her a smile that looked a lot like her own, like her hair and her eyes—if there hadn't been three years between them they could have been twins.

Nadine flicked back the wisps of her auburn-tinted brown hair. 'How's it going anyway? Are you finding everything okay? Taking notes for every call? Being polite?' She dumped the files on to the desk. 'Can you file these while you're hanging round?'

Roxanne rubbed her forehead to ease the pain and sat up straighter. 'Sure, but shouldn't you be at home with Rory? I've got this all covered.'

Her sister scooped up the papers from a tray on her desk. 'I've got a sitter with her for an hour so I haven't

got much time...I just wanted to catch up on paperwork... Are you sure you're all right with this? I know
I sort of dropped this on you, but you *were* jobless...'

Roxanne stood up. 'I'm fine. Everything's fine. I'm
handling everything. I've had plenty of experience in
office management.'

Nadine nodded, heading for the door. 'Not this kind
of office, I'll bet.'

Roxanne's mind shot to the scene earlier in the bar.
That was for sure.

'And I forgot to tell you, if there's anyone who
can't wait until next week just pass them on to the
private investigators that I wrote there in the appointment book.'

Roxanne's gaze wandered over to the number
scrawled on the top of the book. Just great. She could
have told her *that* earlier.

The elegant woman had come in first thing this
morning, insisting on getting the job done at the
soonest possible time, threatening to take her business
elsewhere if Roxanne couldn't guarantee an immedi-
ate start.

'And ring me if there's a problem at all; I can track
down a sitter for Rory for an hour or so while she's
sleeping. I can be a mother and troubleshoot messes
at the same time.'

Roxanne froze. *Her* messes. She could hear
Nadine's accusation as clearly in her tone as every

other time that her sister had come and saved the day for her, whether she wanted saving or not.

Since their mother had passed away Nadine had taken over the role with a vengeance. Well, she wasn't a teenager any more and Nadine didn't need to know she'd gone and tried to do a job herself and made a mess of it.

So, she had messed up the first time. She wasn't going to run to Nadine at the first sign of trouble, she wasn't going to pass the buck and she certainly wasn't going to show that she wasn't prepared to go out there in the real world again and put herself on the market.

She could face Cade Taylor Watson again.

Roxanne was up to the task, just not today, not without some more preparation and planning. She'd blundered in earlier, but not again.

She straightened the papers on the desk with quick, jerky movements, avoiding her sister's gaze. Saying no to that client wouldn't have been good for Nadine's business anyway and the business was all her sister had after her jerk of a husband ran off with his secretary.

Nadine had taken up where her ex's investigating business had left off. She didn't just do the general private investigating work that her husband had done with a few marital jobs thrown in. Marital was her speciality.

Roxanne was behind the idea of testing a man's fidelity one hundred and fifty per cent. She wished she'd known about it years ago—her life would have been so different if she had.

Nadine yanked open the door. 'So, call me if you have any problems. In the meantime, just make appointments and take messages.'

Roxanne nodded, clamping down on the urge to confess her foray earlier. 'I'm here to help,' she blurted, plastering a smile on her face.

She would have come to help her sister earlier, but she had been committed elsewhere, in another state, with her own life, job, apartment and lover...

Now, she wasn't.

She should have come as soon as she heard Nadine was starting up her own business and saved herself a lot of distress instead of staying in Melbourne.

'How's Rory?' Roxanne blurted. If her daughter hadn't been sick Nadine would have been here when the client had come in. She would have known exactly what to do and how to pull it off without a hitch, first time round. 'Better?'

'Not really.' Her sister glanced behind her, frowning. 'I've got to get back just in case she wakes up and needs me.'

Roxanne nodded.

'And don't hide here all night. You have to have a life too. You've got to put your chin up and get on with it, you know.'

She held her tongue as her sister swept out, closing the door firmly behind her. There was nothing wrong with staying late at work. It didn't mean anything. She was *so* over Aaron.

Her belly twisted at the thought of him, of what he could be doing—whether he thought of her at all, or not.

She lifted her chin. She had a problem to solve and she had a duty to *not* distract Nadine from her daughter. They needed time together and her niece needed her mother more than her mother needed to worry about work.

That was her job, for now, and she was going to manage the office and keep the place ticking over until Nadine got back, and she was going to do it no matter what it took, even baiting handsome men.

If, in the process, she managed to prove to her sister that she wasn't the total cock-up that she thought she was, it would be a bonus. Sure, she was useless in keeping a relationship with a guy, keeping a house tidy and keeping a fridge sanitary, but she could do this.

If someone wanted to prove that Cade Taylor Watson was a womaniser, a man likely to roam, a man who was going to betray his girlfriend, then she was the woman for the job.

She wasn't a quitter.

She was going to nail the guy.

She couldn't help but smile, the vision of Cade Taylor Watson's handsome face coming to mind.

Her body warmed. Who could call it work?

All she had to do was get him to show his true colours... How hard could it be? He was a man.

The job was as good as done.

CHAPTER THREE

THE restaurant was perfect. The lighting soft, the twinkling candles on the tables, the gentle strains of the lone lute player filling the room, curling around her.

The mood was gentle, romantic, inviting love, inviting intimacy...cripes, inviting sex. She couldn't have done it better.

Roxanne swivelled on the barstool, surveying the patrons leaning in to each other in whispered closeness.

She had plenty of time. If he got here at a reasonable hour...and the word was that a call was going to come in with the message that suggested his fiancée couldn't make it. He'd think there'd be plenty of time to explore his options with her, and for her to prove his infidelity.

The guy didn't stand a chance.

She smoothed down her indecently tight red gown. She had considered a short one that showed a lot of leg but she decided classy elegance would be better in this case, knowing Cade a little better.

Roxanne caught herself. Not that she knew him. Goodness, a couple of seconds and a smile didn't mean a thing.

Sure, she'd pored over the information that she had been given on him. The fact that he had two parents who were still in love after thirty-five years, that he had a younger sister in the art business, that he had an apartment on the north side with views of the bay and was a top architect and partner in a prominent firm in Sydney. They were just facts. So, the guy liked to go camping, fishing and to all sorts of theatre. It wasn't like knowing this information meant anything, least of all that she was interested.

This was not a dating service—it was a fidelity-testing one to see whether the guy was marriage material for Miss Heather Moreton or not, to give a guarantee that most wanted when committing to a guy, but rarely got.

This was an amazing service that her sister offered her clients so they didn't have to go through all that pain later. And it would come.

Men couldn't be trusted. Not an inch, no matter how nice and kind and handsome they appeared to be. Men were all the same. Liars, who'd betray to serve their own interests when you least expected it.

She couldn't help but think of her mother, her sister and a myriad of friends…

Roxanne gripped the bar stool.

Cade Taylor Watson strode through the door, his black suit hugging his generous frame, his white shirt throwing the deep purple tie he wore in stark contrast, and his presence striking her immediately.

Hell.

He could have been wearing a tuxedo for the cut of the suit, the commanding aura he exuded as he strode towards her…the bar.

She swung back around, staring at her tropical daiquiri, her mind blank.

What was her line for meeting him again? Fate? It seemed so stupid now…maybe he wouldn't even recognise her from last time. He probably hadn't given her a second thought over the weekend…

What she'd said to him had haunted her, as did her foolish move to rush in without looking at her watch, thinking of nothing but talking to the guy, touching base, making a connection and hoping and praying that he was interested in her and she wasn't making the biggest fool of herself for talking to him.

The only difference in doing this job opposed to real dating was that she was getting paid…or at least Nadine was.

He took a stool one space away. 'Scotch, neat,' he directed the barman, plucking his pen from his shirt pocket.

She focused all her attention on her glass. Did he want her number? Already?

The umbrella in her drink was pink, sticking out at a wild angle, the straws standing tall and straight, the multitude of fruit stuck to the side of the glass testament to her avoidance of any alcohol this time, not until it was over. She couldn't afford to take any risks.

It was her last chance. There was no way even the stupidest guy could imagine a chance meeting happening *three* times.

She adjusted the purse balancing on her lap, pushing down the button on the tape recorder. It probably would have been better to have hidden a camera somewhere but she had no idea how to use the one from the office, and from what Nadine said it had cost a fortune.

Roxanne straightened the umbrella and plucked a strawberry off the side of her glass, biting down on the soft flesh of the fruit, trying to think above the roaring blood in her head.

Wasn't he going to say anything?

Did he remember her?

The silence between them stretched.

She felt a twinge of disappointment. Why couldn't it have been easy?

She moved her glass, knocking her napkin off the bar. 'Oh,' she breathed, turning slightly and watching it flutter to the floor.

Cade looked up from the napkin he was doodling on, cast a look down at hers and bent down, snatching it with his long fingers. He lifted it and his gaze to her. 'You dropped this—'

She met his golden eyes, a smile creeping unbidden to her lips at the surprise in them.

Point one for his act of surprise.

He handed her the napkin, his gaze skittering over

her. 'Aren't you the woman with the cute pick-up line last Friday night at Harry's?'

She nodded.

'What did you say?' he said, narrowing his eyes and pointing his pen at her.

She lifted a hand. 'Oh, no. Don't—' The last thing she wanted was to revisit that embarrassment.

'That I'd been in your dreams?' he offered warmly, his gaze fixed on her face.

She shook her head, trying to laugh. 'Okay, now it sounds ten times more corny than it did then.'

He laid the napkin on the bar, swinging his stool to face hers. 'Fancy meeting you here.'

'Yes.' What else could she say? Certainly not the corny line she'd rehearsed about fate.

Cade rubbed his jaw, as though warring with himself. 'Look, I'm sorry about leaving so abruptly.'

She waved her hands to stop him. There was no need to get down on tape that particular disaster. 'What are you drinking? Can I buy you a drink?'

The barman delivered his Scotch. 'Mr Taylor Watson?'

Cade glanced at the guy. 'Yes.'

'Message for you,' the barman said, handing him a piece of paper.

Cade scanned the paper.

This was it. The message regarding his fiancée, saying she'd had to cancel on him, leaving him free to explore her…

She crossed her fingers on her lap, sending a prayer upward. This had to work. 'Can I buy you that drink?'

Cade brandished his glass. 'Thanks, but look, I'm sort of attached…'

Roxanne's chest tightened. What now? Did that win him the grand prize of Heather Moreton?

She wasn't used to this. This wasn't her. She'd never initiated a date or anything with a guy. She'd taken the easy route, waiting until they showed interest in her and she was in the position of saying yes or no to them, not this way round.

She wasn't good with rejection.

'I hear the restaurant is good here,' she offered, swinging back to her drink and taking a gulp. Better that she look uncommitted to the outcome…and better make sure that she appeared to have the message loud and clear, on tape.

Solid proof for the client.

'Yes, it's one of the best,' he said easily. 'The spinach and feta cannelloni is extremely nice…it's my favourite.'

She turned to him, daring to look at the guy again. What the heck. If she wasn't going to go all out tonight and test the man, she never would. 'I love Italian.'

'Me too.'

A silence descended between them. He seemed happy to sit quietly with his drink while she tortured herself over what in heaven she'd say next to get the job done right.

'Nice weather we're having,' she offered, her cheeks heating annoyingly, lifting her gaze to meet his as the book said to do.

'Yes.' He smiled. 'If we're lucky it'll rain all week while we work and be sunny for the weekend.'

'You have plans?' she blurted. 'For the weekend?' She glanced back at her drink and started plucking the rest of the fruit off the rim. 'Not that I'm thinking of going wherever you do to initiate another very embarrassing conversation with a total stranger...'

He laughed. 'I can't say I thought that for a moment. There's an exhibition at the gallery in the city with photos of architectural periods in the twentieth century.'

Roxanne nodded, thankful for the rescue from a fit of babbling that she could have drowned herself in. 'Sounds interesting. I like the baroque period myself, but I'm guessing it's a bit old to make it in.'

He raised his brows, nodding. 'There are some baroque-like influences in the twentieth century architecture. There's that building in the city—' He stopped short, jerking his attention to his glass, swirling the contents.

She leant towards him. 'What?'

He looked up, meeting her gaze. 'Sorry. I get carried away.'

The urge to touch his arm was incredible. She figured that Nadine would have without hesitating, to test the guy, but she was frozen in her seat. 'I'm interested,' she said quietly. 'You're into architecture?'

'I'm an architect.' He offered his hand to her. 'Cade.'

'Roxanne,' she said, joining her hand with his large strong one, slipping her fingers around his palm, absorbing the warmth and the strange tingling sensation.

'And what do you do?' he asked, wrapping his fingers around hers and holding.

Roxanne moistened her lips, fighting to stay focused. 'I'm an office manager. Usually I work for small companies like real estate agents but at the moment—' She caught herself. Idiot. How could she forget why she was here?

She stared at where her hand was still encompassed by his, his warmth slowly working its way up her arm and spreading through her like sunshine on a winter's day.

Even if he appeared nice and kind now, he was still a man, like every other man, and would disappoint Miss Moreton…

She met his golden gaze. 'At the moment I'm fine-tuning my skills at creating embarrassing silences, dishing out corny pick-up moments and collecting incredibly sad and pathetic rejections from really nice guys…who are already attached.'

'What can I say?' he murmured softly, the deep rumble of his voice echoing through her as he deftly pulled his hand back. 'I'm incredibly flattered by your corny pick-up line and the fact that you'd go out of your way to offer it to me. That takes a lot of courage, you know.'

She nodded and took a long drink from her glass, savouring the sweetness and the bite that would make her feel better. 'I know.'

'I haven't noticed any embarrassing silences... The quiet moments in our conversation have been opportunities for me to contemplate how beautiful you are and how many men would fall over backwards to get the sort of attention you've shown me.' He leaned forward a little. 'Can I ask, why do you feel you need to make the first move? You can't be short of offers.'

Roxanne stared at him, his words melting over her. He thought she was beautiful? And what was it with him being so nice? This was all wrong.

'That's sweet of you, and I'm not short of offers,' she said smoothly, ignoring the chaos inside her. 'Just short of the right guys offering.' She closed her eyes on the vision of a plethora of men and their propositions flooding in on her and just how many had turned into disasters.

She opened her eyes, meeting Cade Taylor Watson's fine golden eyes that were watching her with a tenderness that belied his words.

Would it be out of the question to keep him if Heather didn't?

She blinked and took another large gulp of her

drink. Where had that come from? 'And are you committed to someone special,' she blurted, trying one
more time for the *coup de grâce*, 'or are you just
attached tonight and you're mostly single, available
and looking for a date for the photo exhibition?'

'I have a date.'

'But—' She could feel the icy fingers of rejection
sliding through her again, and she didn't want it, not
yet. She wasn't ready to end this conversation with
Cade and give in to the fact that he was actually nice
and Miss Moreton could go ahead and marry him. 'I
like you,' she blurted.

Cade glanced at his watch and stood up, looking
down at her, his face sober. 'I like you too.'

This was it. She mentally crossed her fingers and
toes, willing the outcome she was paid to get.

'You're a lovely person and I could always do with
another friend,' he offered, his tone soft.

'Story of my life,' she murmured. He was the perfect gentleman. She closed her eyes, imagining how
thrilled the client would be at the news, fighting the
odd sensation trying to smother her.

She'd wanted him to choose her.

If Cade Taylor Watson had chosen *her* everything
would have been okay. She could keep going in life
knowing men couldn't be trusted and make her decisions accordingly. Now she was confused about everything except the fact that Heather Moreton was one
lucky woman.

Roxanne felt him stiffen beside her.

She looked up.

His fiancée stood in the doorway, the woman who had his loyalty and his heart.

'Good luck,' he said, offering her a small consolatory smile. 'With everything.'

'You too,' she whispered. When was *she* going to find a man like that to love her with such loyalty and commitment?

Roxanne watched Cade Taylor Watson saunter over to the love of his life, who was watching her with narrowed eyes.

She took a deep, slow breath and nodded, shooting Heather a thumbs up. She was one lucky girl to be marrying a man like that.

Roxanne drank the rest of her cocktail and stood up. The job was over and done with and not a minute too soon. She was getting far too involved in the charade for her own good.

How Heather could even have doubted him was beyond her; Cade was one hell of a guy.

She looked up to the ceiling and put her order in, and the sooner the better. She needed some happiness in her life too.

She only hoped there was another man like him out there for her.

CHAPTER FOUR

ROXANNE sat behind the desk in Nadine's office, back straight, chin up and eyes forward, counting down the minutes until the client arrived.

She could hear the woman's high heels on the stairs, could almost hear what she was thinking about the state of the place, the lighting and the lack of paint on the walls in the hall as she came in.

Roxanne flattened down her hair, straightened her shirt collar and placed her hands calmly on the desk. It was time to get this over with, and she wasn't in any hurry to get into this situation again. Nadine may be suited to the task of testing men, but not her. She was happy to stay in the office where she was safe.

The door opened. Roxanne forced a gentle smile to her face. 'Good morning, Miss Moreton.'

'Save it. Just tell me…did you get the dirt on him?' she barked.

Roxanne stared at Cade's elegant fiancée. Her three-piece trouser suit was as light as her skin, as pressed and flawless as her hair and as expensive as the jewellery that glittered at her neck, ears and wrists, including an incredible diamond on her ring finger. Cade's ring.

Roxanne crossed her arms over her chest. 'Have you considered for a moment that he may be the kind, upstanding, loyal man he appears to be?'

'I didn't pay you to find that out.' She stalked across the room, made a cursory appraisal of the velvet-padded chair and sat down gingerly on it. 'I paid you to tempt him and I have to say that your red slinky dress was a nice touch. He didn't stand a chance.'

'Again, you assume that the man isn't faithful to you.' Roxanne rearranged the pens on the desk, annoyed at the woman's attitude. It was almost as though she *wanted* him to have cheated on her. 'I gave you the thumbs up signal,' she suggested lightly. Had she assumed she'd meant the worst?

'Yes, I saw…because you got the result.'

'I got *a* result, yes.' Roxanne shook her head. 'I have to ask, are you just terribly insecure about your own worth…because I'm sure there are attributes that you have that Cade loves you for.'

Roxanne held her breath, watching the woman consider her question, her pinched mouth and drawn brow sending a sliver of concern sliding through her. *Maybe she didn't.* Apart from being impeccably neat, with the style of a model and the looks of one… she probably didn't think she had much else, but Cade obviously did.

Heather waved a hand impatiently. 'I did not employ you to be a counsellor. I employed you to test my fiancé and find out if he deserves me.'

Roxanne chilled at the woman's harsh tone and foregone conclusion. 'You seem to have already made up your mind about him. Can I ask why? Do you have suspicions? A reason not to trust him?'

The woman lit up a cigarette. 'He's a man, isn't he?'

'Not all men are the same,' Roxanne blurted, biting her tongue. Was that her talking? After Aaron and David and Steve...

The woman lifted a finely crafted eyebrow. 'Look, if it's a question of money I'm quite willing to pay more if you need more time to fashion yourself to be just the sort of woman he'd look sideways at. Or if you feel that the job you've already done—and which you're dragging out—is worth more. Fine, I'll pay it, just tell me he's a lying cheat.'

Roxanne stared at the papers in front of her, shuffling them dutifully, knowing full well the only evidence she had was of the man being nice, caring and wonderful, if not a little too kind to strange women at bars.

Miss Moreton stood up, glaring down at her. 'The wedding is in less than two weeks. Two weeks! Have you any idea how much organisation is in a wedding? How much it costs? How much pressure there is? You have to give me something...anything...'

'If you've got cold feet, maybe you should discuss it with your fiancé,' Roxanne suggested, tipping her head and trying to make the woman out. It seemed that she only wanted one outcome and that was all she would accept. 'Rather than go this way.'

The woman stared icily at her. 'Again, not your business, just tell me what I want to know.'

'Okay.' Roxanne lifted the file from beside her, the tape she'd made sitting under it. 'As you know, I've had two encounters with your fiancé and I don't feel anything more would be gained from another.'

She toyed with the tape. If only she hadn't been paid to meet with him. 'I have the conversation recorded for verification.'

Heather snatched the tape off her and stowed it in her bag. She paused, looked up and smiled. 'I'm paying for it, aren't I?'

Roxanne froze. The tape… the actual evidence of what *didn't* go down. 'The tape *is* quite general. He *appears* to be a complete gentleman in everything he says and does,' she said carefully, wondering how to break the news that Cade appeared to be everything a woman could want in a man.

'But—' Miss Moreton leant her palms heavily on the desk, staring down at Roxanne with eyes blazing. 'God help me. Tell me there's a *but*. I've got thirteen days until the wedding. Give me a reason not to marry the man.'

She stared blankly at the woman. 'Okay.' Roxanne jerked to her feet, her blood heating at the ridiculousness of the situation. This woman had a really nice guy and she didn't want him while there were a multitude of women out there struggling to find just that.

Darn it. The woman didn't want the truth…she only wanted to hear that Cade was a cheat.

What did he see in her? Was this the real woman and he was some masochist or was she two-faced and had taken the poor guy for a ride?

She couldn't imagine Cade with anyone who wasn't nice…

Roxanne lifted her chin. Well, she would darned well give the woman what she wanted.

She thrust the file across the desk with an invoice for her time. 'The man had bedroom eyes,' Roxanne blurted, meeting the client's cold hard gaze, knowing that the tape could in no way show it. 'And the sexiest mouth that he used to his advantage—though not a crime…'

What was she doing?

Giving Heather Moreton what she wanted, what the client wanted, and what every single woman in Sydney would want her to do to free up another nice guy.

'He sat so close to me his fresh soap and spicy cologne filled my senses—' She paused and took a deep breath, closing her eyes. 'And he was radiating pure hot male just waiting for the right woman to come and sate his lust.'

Miss Moreton straightened tall. 'So he *did* proposition you?' she said, her face softening.

Roxanne wet her dry lips, her mind filling with visions of what it would have been like with him if Heather hadn't been his fiancée.

She glanced at the client who was nodding enthusiastically, her face all smiles at the supposed revelation. Would Miss Moreton hear the truth if she actually listened to the tape in her bag? Probably not with the prejudice she seemed to have.

'He all but invited me to a gallery,' she said, finding it easier to embellish the truth knowing it was what the client wanted.

Cripes, Heather almost looked ecstatic at the news. 'He teased me with his schedule, probably in the hopes that I'd hook up with him later.' She bit her lip, trying to stop herself.

'What else?' Heather barked.

She wanted more? 'And he failed to mention his engagement to you,' she said in a rush. 'And I have to say that we really had a connection, and if you hadn't come in when you did we probably would have…spent the night together.'

She looked away, embarrassed at the insinuation she'd given. Sure, they would have. He was easy to talk to and she was sure they *could* have talked all night, but Heather Moreton probably didn't *want* to know that.

Miss Moreton nodded, a thin smile stretching across her face. 'Good. Good.' She gave the invoice a glance, bent over and wrote a cheque, her grin widening. 'I should have known you were a professional. I was a bit worried last week but you came through.'

'Here to help,' Roxanne said tightly. This was absolutely crazy. The man was a saint and a wonderful guy…but if this woman didn't see that, didn't want to see that, then she didn't deserve him.

Cade deserved true love and happiness, not to be married to a witch who didn't even want him.

She leant back in her seat watching the woman, with her perfect head held high and her grin a mile wide, straighten up and saunter out of the office.

Roxanne then stared at the cheque on the desk, gnawing on her bottom lip. She *had* done the world a favour. She'd saved a really nice guy from a fate worse than death and liberated a bachelor for some grateful woman somewhere who'd treasure him.

She didn't know what Heather Moreton's problem was, but it was solved now. For better or for worse, Cade was free.

Cade leant against his car, waiting for Heather. It wasn't typical for her to change their plans, let alone bring them forward. Backward, yes. She'd done that a fair bit over the past few weeks, but she'd never made it sooner.

He rubbed his jaw. She probably just wanted to talk about the wedding. The last-minute plans, including whether he'd done his bit in organising the honeymoon. She needn't have worried. He had it all covered.

Maybe she wanted to talk about Roxanne.

He'd felt all last night through the meal the weight of the unsaid between them. It didn't feel right that she could ignore what had happened.

She'd had every opportunity to question his affection for her after seeing him with Roxanne at the bar, the same woman she'd seen him with the other day.

Did she trust him that much?

Did she love him that blindly?

Hell, he *was* a fool. How could he doubt his own affection for his fiancée now...when she was obviously so in love with him, and just weeks before the wedding?

She loved him.

It was in everything she did. The time she spent with him and his friends. The time she took out of her busy schedule to visit his family. The time she was taking away from him to make their special day unforgettable.

How could he even spend a moment thinking about the woman in red at the bar?

He sighed. He couldn't believe how the communication between him and Heather had gone awry that day. He was sure her message had been that she couldn't make it. Then she'd turned up out of the blue.

She must love him so much to get out of some

meeting to spend time with him. And he was making an idiot out of himself.

Maybe it was just cold feet. Nerves. The last fantasy of an engaged man…with under a fortnight to go until he walked down the aisle.

He sucked in a deep breath and pushed down his negative thoughts. He should concentrate on spending all the time he could with Heather, focusing on her needs, helping her with their wedding plans and being her rock.

She was doing so much for them both, and the time she spent away from him was probably as hard on her as it was for him…when they needed to spend time together and affirm their connection.

He crossed his arms and leant back, leaning on his car, surveying the basement garage of Heather's apartment complex. She'd probably realised it herself and needed to see him tonight…for him to hold her and tell her how much he wanted to marry her, for her to tell him how much she loved him.

Cade sighed. No doubts and no distractions would be nice until the wedding, but he knew that life rarely worked like that.

It had been a funny thing to meet that stunning woman again. He'd thought meeting a woman like that last week had been special, fated, a sweet reminder of all the things he had to look forward to with Heather, once they were married.

He'd wondered about her all weekend, considering

what the story might be behind her making the first move.

There was no reason why a woman that beautiful had to go putting herself on the line to find nice men. Hell, were nice men blind?

To meet the mystery woman again had been surreal. She was so different. Intriguing. And damned hard to get out of his mind.

'Cade,' Heather barked, striding towards him, stunning in a white three-piece suit, her hair curled up and her lips pulled thin.

Cade frowned. He'd never heard that tone before— hard and icy—she must have had a rough day and needed him all the more.

'Heather.' He opened his arms for her warm embrace but she stopped two paces too short, her face sober, her eyes narrowed. 'What's wrong?'

She grasped the engagement ring he'd given her, yanked it off her finger and held it out to him, her palm flat. 'I'm afraid the engagement is off.'

'Off?' he echoed, peeling himself off his car and standing tall, staring at the ring in her hand, his mind tumbling around for the significance in her words. Was she being serious?

'Off,' she snapped, shoving the ring into his jacket pocket and shrinking back as though she was loath to touch him. 'I don't want to marry you any more.'

'Why?' He touched the ring in his pocket. Everyone

had convinced them that they were perfect for each other, their parents, their friends…

Didn't she love him any more?

She crossed her arms and expelled a rush of air. 'Because I can't trust you.'

'What?' He tossed the ridiculous notion over and around but couldn't figure it out. 'I've never given you cause or reason—'

She lifted her finely arched eyebrows and sneered. 'Does the woman in the red dress last night ring any bells?'

'What about her?' His voice caught in his throat. Had she jumped to conclusions over the coincidence of him being at a bar with her again? Did she guess how intrigued he was by her? Was it written on his face?

'I know all about her,' she said hotly. 'I know how you wanted to take her home and tear her clothes off and make mad passionate love with her all over your apartment.'

Mad passionate love with the woman in red? What a thought…sweeping her long reddy-brown hair off her shoulder, touching his lips to her warm skin, tracing her curves with his hands…

He shook his head.

This couldn't be happening. How could it? Nothing had happened. Sure, he'd fantasized a bit about the girl, but he was getting married. He was entitled to a couple of fantasies, wasn't he? 'Nothing happened, nothing *would* happen.'

Heather stabbed the air in front of him. 'That's not what I hear.'

He frowned. What? 'From where, from who?' He prided himself on doing the right thing. How could anyone accuse him of doing the wrong thing? He would never do anything to hurt her...

Heather swung away from him. 'I've got a witness...who was very particular about what went on before I arrived to find you talking intimately with *her*.'

'What witness?'

She glared at him. 'My family loves me anyway. They won't want me marrying a lying womaniser.'

'The witness is one of your family?' Cade ran a hand through his hair. 'You can't believe them. It wasn't how it looked.'

She nodded solemnly. 'It's over. It was a mistake. I never want to see you again.'

Cade stared at the woman he had been sure he was going to marry. 'The wedding—?'

'I expect you to cover all costs...' She choked, covering her mouth, avoiding his gaze. 'I'll let everyone know what's happened.'

He stared at her, unable to find the words to express the fear rushing through him. 'But,' he muttered, fighting with the memory of Roxanne, what he felt about the mysterious stranger... 'But nothing happened.

This is silly.' He looked to the roof of the garage. 'If there's another reason why you don't want to marry me...'

She held her head up, her eyes blazing. 'You have the gall to accuse *me* when you betrayed me with that woman? Do I need another reason other than you're not the man I thought you were?' She turned away. 'Goodbye, Cade.'

Cade stared after her as she stalked back into her apartment building. How could talking to a woman, albeit a pretty one, constitute betrayal? Her family was wrong...her witness was wrong. Maliciously trying to hurt the woman he was engaged to. Ruin his wedding. Ruin his life.

He was innocent. And he was going to find that woman in red and prove it. No matter what it took.

CHAPTER FIVE

'WILL you be dining alone?'

Roxanne nodded, unable to look up at the waiter. It felt weird, but she was determined. If she could chat a complete stranger up in a bar and discover a really decent guy, then she could go out for a meal by herself.

She didn't need a man to take her out to eat somewhere nice. She was going to be strong, independent, get on with her life and put the past behind her.

So what if she'd had more than several failed relationships, it was what life was about. Trying guys on. The fact that she couldn't get one to fit so perfectly that there were no doubts at all about him…

She glanced around the restaurant, at the bar where she'd met Cade the second time, the last time…

It didn't mean anything that she'd come here; she had to eat and tonight she was thinking Italian. Why ignore the best place to eat?

Cade Taylor Watson would be okay…maybe he'd even sorted through whatever problems he and Heather had that drove her to seek the aid of her sister's company.

Had he already wandered? Had they had a break

and he'd taken the opportunity to sow some wild and passionate oats in some welcoming field?

Probably…

She spread the napkin over her black trousers. It sort of felt weird to ask for a table for one…she had never gone to a restaurant alone. Sure, takeaway for one. A hotdog on the run for one, pizza for one…but this was a first.

She straightened the setting in front of her with the odd sensation that she was being watched by everyone in the room, as though she was a walking invitation for pity.

She sat taller, straightening her white office shirt. She was a woman declaring her independence, making a stand for all single women out there with poor judgement of men and even worse decisions.

Roxanne took the menu, perusing the offerings. It was filled with indulgent Italian dishes, rich with herbs and cheese and garlic… She scanned down the list.

What was she doing here? Really? Was it to somehow assuage the guilt that was clawing at her every time she stopped and thought about Cade and what she'd done?

She gnawed at the nail on the end of her index finger, running through her reasons again in her head and that last encounter with Heather that assured her that she'd done the right thing.

Goodness, she had had every intention of telling the

woman her fiancé was a very nice man until Miss Moreton had insisted on only accepting the opposite.

She may not have done the correct thing but she'd done the right thing, for both of them.

That woman was obviously finding an excuse to dump the guy. He could do way better, and the single realm was far better off to have him in it.

Roxanne fiddled with the napkin, glancing around the room, at the couples nestled intimately, many in close conversation.

She looked down at her lap, at the white cloth spread across her legs, smoothing the fabric with her palms. She wouldn't ever be able to look at a napkin again without thinking of Cade, of his doodles and what she'd done.

Cripes. What gave her the right to interfere? It was ridiculous to presume she'd know what was best for that man, when she couldn't even work out her own life.

She didn't want to think about it, and didn't have to. That chapter in her life was well and truly over. It was time to spend some quality time with her family and, with Nadine back at work, there was no need for her to go out in the field again, ever.

Roxanne was going to enjoy Nadine and Rory and some off the shelf time where she didn't have to think about men at all. She'd been through enough.

She smiled, putting down the menu. No men. It sounded good. She looked up at the waiter hovering beside the table. 'I'd like the cannelloni and a garden salad and a glass of your house red.'

She surveyed the room again, watching the flickering candles on the tables and listening to the soft strains of another lute player adding to the mood.

It was a carbon copy of the other night, except *she'd* been at that bar… She looked across and scanned the patrons perched on the stools, the men in dark suits, one in particular looking a lot like the squared shoulders of Cade Taylor Watson.

She shook herself, turning her attention to the cutlery in front of her—she was seeing him everywhere. She'd thought she'd seen him in a hundred places over the last three days, but it had always turned out to be someone else.

Not that she was looking or wondering about the guy. He was the sort of guy who would take it on the chin and get on with life, find a woman who would adore him and love him and want to spend as much time with him as she possibly could.

She wouldn't mind a guy as kind and as friendly and as easy coming into *her* life.

Yes. A handsome, kind and considerate professional who knew where to buy clothes and what tailor would best accentuate his attributes. Not a big ask, but not for now. For now, she was having a break.

One thing she knew for sure, there was no point in putting Cade Taylor Watson on her wish list. A man a lot like him, definitely, but not him. There was no way she could see *him* again.

The waiter paused by her table, a colourful daiquiri in his hand. 'A gentleman at the bar would like to offer you a drink.'

She took a quick breath, the irony sliding through her at the gesture that she'd used to pick Cade up, the flush of embarrassment new on her cheeks. 'I'm sorry, could you tell the gentleman—'

'You can tell him yourself,' a deep male voice said beside her.

His tone hit her, the jolt of familiarity igniting her senses. It couldn't be—

Roxanne swung around, looking up and meeting Cade Taylor Watson's golden eyes. 'I—'

All thought left her mind.

She could only stare.

He looked great. A dark suit hugged his wide shoulders, a silky blue tie knotted neatly against a white shirt, he looked as if he'd come straight from the office, right down to the five o'clock shadow on his jaw.

The waiter put the drink on the table in front of her. 'Would the gentleman be dining with the lady?'

'That would be up to the lady,' Cade said easily, holding the chair opposite hers, poised as though ready to pull it out and sit down.

She looked up at the man. All she could do was stare; her throat had closed over and her mind spun. What was he doing here? Had Heather Moreton dumped him for his supposed infidelity yet? Or had he been waiting for her and tonight was going to be the night?

Alarm bells rang.

She glanced towards the door, yanked the fruit off the glass in front of her and gulped down some of the sweet fruity mix, waiting for the kick.

'I—' she tried, putting the glass down and staring at the man pulling the chair out from the table and sitting down in it.

'I'm so glad I've finally found you,' he said, arranging the cutlery as though she'd agreed, the waiter following suit, setting his place. 'I knew it was a long shot because although the barmen remembered you— you're not easy to forget—they both said they hadn't seen you before and didn't know who you were or have a clue where to find you. And I've been sitting at Harry's every afternoon watching for you and every night coming here in the hope of finding you.'

Roxanne's mind seized. Why? Her blood rushed to her head, roaring in her ears and filling her cheeks with fire.

Why was he here? Had Heather Moreton told him everything and he'd come to strangle her for interfering in his life?

Cade leant an arm on the table. 'I need to ask you a favour.'

She stared at him, her mind fighting to understand his words, his gentle tone, his kind warm eyes looking at her as though he didn't have an ounce of animosity towards her.

'I know that you can put my fiancée's mind at rest,' he said softly.

'Why?' she asked cautiously, toying with the possibilities. What had Heather said to him?

He sat back in his chair. 'Because she's decided the wedding's off because I spoke to you.' He flicked the button open on his jacket and ran his hands through his short hair. 'She's got it into her head that I intended to—'

'Yes, well.' Roxanne took another sip of the drink. She could imagine Heather not holding back at all on that particular subject.

The waiter offered Cade a menu.

Cade shook his head. 'Not necessary. I'll have the same as the lady.'

She stirred her drink with the little plastic stick, her order haunting her. Did he know that she'd ordered what he'd recommended? That she had been thinking of him? Had been haunted by him?

'The drink's okay?' he asked, sitting forward and leaning his elbows on the table.

'Great. It's my favourite—' She caught herself, pausing. 'How did you know what I drink?' Had she made an impression on him, besides being the instrument that had ruined his engagement?

'I remembered, and so did the barman.' He smiled

sheepishly at her. 'You have quite an effect on people.'

She had to look away. If only he knew.

She focused on her drink but was acutely aware of him watching her. She wanted to straighten her hair, wished she'd touched up her make-up, hoped her white shirt was still as white as when she'd put it on this morning and that her suit didn't look as off-the-rack and ordinary as it so obviously was.

He leant forward on the table. 'So was I your first?'

She jerked her head up, cold tendrils slicing through her belly and down her spine. Had he found out that she'd been virgin bait, a first time investigator, a novice? 'How did you know?' she choked.

'It was obvious.' A smile tugged at the corners of his mouth as though he was amused by her surprise. 'The book sort of gave it away.'

She stared at him, numb.

'I figured once you'd got comfortable in a few places you'd keep going to them to try out your pick-up lines and independence, though I was terrified that someone else had taken up your offer and whisked you off.'

His words seeped into her like conditioner into knots, easing the tangle of fear. He didn't know the truth. 'It does happen occasionally,' she said softly, trying to smile.

The waiter placed a glass of red wine in front of each of them and presented a small basket of bread, sliding it on to the edge of the table, the rich aroma of garlic steaming up to meet her.

'I hope I didn't in any way put you off making the first move.' Cade extracted a slice from the basket and surveyed it. 'I think more women should take the initiative in dating rather than sitting on the wall, looking pretty.'

She gazed at him, lost for words, a traitorous buzz running through the entire length of her, down her spine, all the way to her toes. *Did he really think she was pretty?*

'And I was flattered.'

Roxanne stared at him. Making the first move was a nightmare...she certainly had an idea what guys must go through...the fear of rejection alone was incredible... She clenched a fist by her side. She had to learn from this.

'But, I have to say, being on the other end didn't make you consider accepting my drink; you didn't even check out the sender,' he accused in a light tone, pointing to her cocktail. 'I think it would have been nicer if you'd checked me out before refusing it.'

Roxanne stared at the garlic bread. So much for learning to consider a man's feelings... 'I just wasn't in the mood, you know. Hard day at work and all.' And it wasn't as if she hadn't checked him out already...

'And what do you do exactly?' he asked, taking a sip of the rich red and plucking out another slice of steaming bread from the basket. 'An office manager, right? For who?'

'I—' she started, her breath tight in her chest. What could she say? Certainly not the truth because there'd be no way she wanted him to be out there in the world thinking badly of her.

'It's not a hard question,' Cade urged, taking another sip of his wine, not taking his eyes off her.

Her mind scrambled. She'd wished for a guy just like him, wanted to spend the night talking to him, needed to let a guy into her life again...and now he was here! But what in heavens was she going to do now?

What could she say?

She had to get rid of this guy or escape, before he found out who she was, or worse, what she'd done.

CHAPTER SIX

HE HAD been lucky to find her.

Cade turned to his plate and picked up his cutlery, glancing at the woman opposite him, who was still flushed from his surprise appearance.

What had been the chances that Roxanne would be in either place again in under a week?

It was fated, like their last visit…

He couldn't help thinking about how that had turned out for him. *He* knew nothing had happened and, okay, he and Roxanne *had* clicked. They could be good friends if the circumstances were different. But that was it.

He wasn't guilty.

Whoever had seen them together had obviously jumped to the wrong conclusion about him talking to a pretty woman who wasn't Heather. It hadn't been Heather who'd made the assumption. If she'd had a problem with him talking to Roxanne again she hadn't said so, wouldn't have needed a witness and would have made her feelings clear to him there and then.

Hell, there was nothing wrong with talking to a nice young woman. And Roxanne had been charming, cute and funny, not to mention downright pretty in that dress of hers. He'd even laughed and he couldn't even remember when he'd last laughed.

He took a mouthful of the rich pasta dish, glancing at Roxanne. She didn't exactly seem thrilled to see him again. Could he have hurt her feelings that night?

Probably.

After all the effort she'd put in to meet him with that book and all, and then to have him discard her so easily when Heather came along… He cringed. Twice. But what else could he have done?

Heather was his fiancée and the fact that she'd been deeply misled and hurt by someone raising accusations against him cut him to the core.

He couldn't understand her so easily believing the lie…

Cade tore his attention away from the delicate way Roxanne was eating the cannelloni, focusing on his own plate, his own problem.

He should have told Heather that talking to Roxanne had just been the friendly thing to do, that it had meant nothing and definitely wasn't meant to hurt her.

He'd never heard Heather be so hard and cold before, or so forceful. But he couldn't imagine the hell she'd been through listening to nasty accusations about him from someone close to her.

Yet how could Heather have believed someone else over him? And cancelling the wedding when everyone had put so much into the preparations? Over him talking to a pretty woman... She must really be deeply hurt.

He had to sort this out.

He slid his knife across the cannelloni. He was going to put things straight for the woman who was going to be his wife, allay her fears, heal her wounds and get their relationship back on track and her down the aisle.

He couldn't believe that she'd give up on them so easily, not when they were so right for each other in every way.

Everyone said so. His mother adored her. His father thought she was sweet and the rest of the clan had fallen all over her. And rightly so; she was adorable.

Cade sighed. There was their future at stake now.

He watched Roxanne, the careful slices she took of the cannelloni, the way she scooped each piece up with her fork, sliding it around her plate to coat it in the thick tomato sauce before taking it to her mouth. And the small sound she made, like a sigh that echoed through his veins.

Watching her eat was like a dance, where all her attention was on her plate.

Cade took a gulp of wine. She almost seemed vulnerable. Unless it was just her total absorption in the flavours. He couldn't blame her. The cannelloni was as good as he remembered.

The chance that she'd ordered it because he'd recommended it felt so damned good. He didn't know why. Heather was never enthusiastic to try something he'd recommended.

He put down his glass, watching Roxanne.

One way or another he'd left an impression on her and he hoped it was a good one. He was starting to suspect it wasn't. He was starting to think that Monday night had been more significant to this woman than just looking for someone nice to be with. She'd needed company, someone to talk to...to be with to build up her confidence in herself again, probably after some nasty break up.

He rubbed his jaw. The woman was beautiful. Who, in his right mind, would break it off with her?

He glanced at her ring finger. Had it been serious? A fiancé or a husband? 'I'm sorry I couldn't stay and talk with you that night,' he offered, his mind scrambling for a way to ask her what he really wanted to know.

She waved a hand in front of her as though she was flicking the words away. 'This cannelloni is incredibly delicious. The flavour is so rich and smooth...' She looked around her, her sea-green eyes flashing. 'I can't imagine why this place isn't overrun.'

He couldn't help but smile at her enthusiasm. 'I'd say that most people aren't as passionate about their Italian food.'

Roxanne took the last mouthful of her cannelloni onto her fork. 'I am.'

'I can tell.'

'What about you? What are you passionate about, apart from your work?' she said in a rush.

Cade leant an elbow on the table. 'I spend a lot of time at the beach. I like to surf.'

'So you have a bit of a beach bum in a business suit thing going?'

'Yes. I fell in love with the beach when I was a kid. Mum and Dad used to drag my sister and I down every weekend in summer.' Cade couldn't help but smile at the memory, of throwing seaweed on his sister and of burying his dad in sand. 'What about you?'

'Yes,' she said softly. 'I love the beach. We sometimes went as a family…'

A soft smile touched her lips and he had the insane urge to lean over and taste it.

He straightened. 'And as you already know I like architecture and I dare to think I know a bit about art,' he said dramatically, watching Roxanne carefully. She was so nice to watch…

'You do, do you? Know all about the impressionists, cubists and sexists?'

'Sexists?'

'It's a new art form I'm working on where jilted lovers shove their exes into large glass boxes surrounded by all their sins.'

He couldn't help but laugh. The woman had been hurt. That was obvious, but she handled it with such class. 'Sounds extremely interesting. Would your family approve?'

Roxanne speared some tomato on her fork. 'Would it matter?'

'I don't like to disappoint my parents.'

'You never know, they could cheer you on.'

Cade's mind darted to his mother walking through a gallery of his exes. Roxanne was right. She'd love it, highlighting the faults of each one. 'It could be a hit, you know. Except for the obvious kidnapping issues.'

She broke into a smile. 'Has anyone told you how utterly charming you are?'

'Are you saying you find me charming?'

'Not if it makes your head grow.'

He swept the scout's oath across his chest. 'Promise I'll keep my head in proportion with the rest of me.'

Her glance swept over him as though she was checking out his proportions. 'I think you're doing okay.'

He laughed to dispel the energy surging through him. 'So are you.'

'I don't think women are in the same risk group as men where big whopping egos are concerned.'

Heather popped into his mind. 'I'm not so sure about that.'

She leant forward, a smile playing on her full red lips. 'Are you saying that I could be under the influence of a big-head?'

'No, but you're one hell of an influence...'

'Right.' A shadow passed over her face.

He put down his cutlery, resisting the urge to steal the last piece of garlic bread to wipe up the pool of rich tomato sauce smearing his plate. 'Look, I want to apologise for the other night again. I suspect you could have needed a shoulder to lean on. Do you want to talk about it?'

'It?'

'Your last relationship,' he offered quietly.

'Oh,' she whispered.

'I figure the other night must have been about more than just the desire to buy me a drink,' he offered, running through the possible explanations that would explain a beautiful woman making the first move.

She wiped her fingers on the napkin and dropped it on to her plate. 'Are you always this nice?'

He shrugged. 'It comes and goes.'

'Well, stop it, okay. Get tough and stop worrying about everyone else and worry about yourself,' she said coolly, avoiding looking directly at him, a flush on her cheekbones.

He narrowed his gaze. 'I don't think there's anything wrong with being a nice guy.'

'Nice guys finish last.'

'What's that supposed to mean?' He reached his hand over the table, covering her small delicate one, trying to assess what was going on, trying to ignore the pull deep in his gut. 'Have I upset you? Can I help?'

Was she okay? And okay enough to ask her again

to meet with Heather and straighten this mess out? Was that too much to ask? To even consider?

The last thing he wanted to do was ask something of her that would torture her more. And he could imagine that talking to a man's fiancée might be one of them.

He knew how obsessed women got over weddings...his younger sister one of them. He'd seen her need for all that white satin, flowers, presents and attention, and the yearning for the groom that would make it all possible. And how it affected her when she figured she was missing out.

'Well, look, I appreciate your concern, your pity, your hanging around to apologise and all that, but—' She stood up, looking at her watch. 'I have to go.'

He pushed back his chair and stood up. Already? She couldn't. He hadn't got any answers, only more questions...

'Roxanne, I didn't spend the last three days waiting around at bars to apologise...' He hesitated, pushing his hands deep into his pockets. 'Okay, maybe I did, but I need you to help me explain to my fiancée what happened the other night.'

She looked towards the door, avoiding his gaze. 'I'm sorry, but we all have our problems...and I can't help... I've nothing left to... I can't. Okay. I just can't.'

He clenched his hands by his sides. Someone had

obviously hurt this woman a lot more than he had first suspected.

'I was wrong. Okay?' she said in a rush. 'I'm sorry. I'm sorry for everything. That first time. The last time. For right now. I'm sorry.'

He looked at her. *Sorry?*

She yanked out some notes from her purse that more than covered the meal for both of them and threw them on to the table. 'I have to go.'

Cade stared after the woman, watching her hips roll in that simple office outfit, suppressing the surge of heat to his loins.

He sighed. He'd upset her again and the realisation made the air tight in his lungs.

All he wanted to do was go after her, make it right, but he was frozen to the spot. She'd obviously had all she could take of him for one night...he'd try again later.

He stiffened. Later...when? When she craved cannelloni? When she deigned to go to a bar and have a daiquiri?

He forced his legs to move. He had to catch her...find out her surname...find out where she lived...worked. He had to find out how in hell he was going to get her to talk to Heather when he couldn't even get her to answer a straight question.

Cade paid for the meal and strode out to find her. She was by the kerb, searching the driveway for the next cab.

'Roxanne,' he said, offering her money to her.

She swung around, her hands tightly clasped in front of her. 'Please, why don't you just accept the inevitable like the rest of us do? Stop fighting it. Just get on with your life, okay?'

He shook his head. Where was the woman he'd met the other night? The optimistic, independent woman who had been keen to meet him, talk to him, buy him a drink and experience life? Who was this enigma?

'You've got your job, your health, your family...and plenty to do.' She pressed her lips together and looked up at him, taking the money he was still holding. 'Work, run, visit your parents and go to plays, exhibitions and galleries.'

'But I've got no date,' he said slowly, watching her face.

'I'm sorry?'

'You can't refuse me.'

She looked taken aback. 'Are you asking?'

He slipped his hands into his pockets. 'I thought I was, but obviously I was doing a bad job at it. I'd love to take you to the gallery tomorrow afternoon... Will you do me the honour of accompanying me so I don't feel like a total loser?'

'Honesty...that's nice.' She smiled softly up at him.

He couldn't help but stare down into her emerald eyes. 'I'm always honest.'

She shook her head, staring at the ground, her cheeks colouring. 'But no.'

He frowned. He couldn't lose her now, not when he was just getting the hint of who she really was. 'As friends, no strings attached?'

She paused.

Was she scared of him? Maybe scared of men in general. Goodness knew what the last man in her life had done to her.

He'd have to find out.

Cade shrugged casually as a cab drove up and stopped next to them. 'I promise I won't ask anything of you at all. Just as friends, enjoying architecture together in a sad and sorry way,' he said slowly, as calmly as he could manage, the breath in his chest threatening to explode at the building pressure there. 'Since we're both on our own.'

'I don't think so,' Roxanne whispered.

'I could do with a friend,' he offered, opening the door of the cab. And he suspected she could too. 'Couldn't you do with one more?'

She sighed and stepped into the cab.

'Don't you feel guilty?'

She jerked her head up, her eyes wide, almost tortured as though he'd touched a raw nerve.

Didn't she have friends? Or had the last man in her life that jerked her around been a friend to her first, before they'd got involved, and then cruelly hurt her?

He gave a soft shrug, trying to relax. 'Please, it's the least you could do since exciting my imagination to the baroque influence in this exhibition. I'd love you to share that with me. You can meet me there if you're more comfortable…?'

'Okay. All right.' She managed a small smile. 'How can I refuse?'

Cade watched the taxi pull away from the kerb, taking note of the number just in case she chickened out and he had to track her down again.

How could he not? Roxanne was the only way to prove his case.

He'd help her fix her life and then she could help him with his. No problem at all.

CHAPTER SEVEN

THE building resembled a square box with a lot of windows, suggesting not much inspiration or imagination. It was quite a contradiction for a gallery, unless they were going for the blank-canvas look where the architecture of the building didn't detract from the work within it.

Roxanne stood in front of the entrance, breathing slowly. She should have stayed at home where it was safe instead of listening to the rumble deep inside, like a hunger that needed to be tended to.

She could have refused his invitation, but guilt had filled her. She had a duty to the man to convince him that Heather wasn't the one for him and to help him let her go and get on with his life.

She owed him that.

She smoothed down the white trousers she wore, straightened her soft pink shirt and lifted her chin. She was going for simply elegant, with light make-up and her hair pulled back, coiled at her nape as she wore it for work.

This was business. An adjunct to the job where she could vindicate herself for her lie and steer Cade in the right direction—well away from Heather and her twisted motives.

She'd keep her distance, highlight his attributes and then disappear. The key was to keep him busy with a list of questions she had on hand about certain Sydney structures.

She had always wanted to know the reason behind the shell-like sails of the Opera House, the tension wires on the Sydney Harbour Bridge and just why there were so many one-way streets in the city.

She approached the entrance, a strange sensation bubbling up from the pit of her stomach at the thought of seeing him again...

What if Cade had found out who she really was and why she'd been at that bar? That it was her who had told his fiancée he wasn't the upstanding gentleman that he was, and she was the one who had helped prove to the lady he wasn't the one for her?

The cold chill of her lie curled inside her, forcing her to keep walking.

Roxanne stared at the building. Sure. She'd be with Cade, but it wasn't like a date. As far as he was concerned it was a just friends sort of thing. He just wanted to be her friend and she just wanted to get this right.

This was just closure for him. Nothing more. It shouldn't take long to make him realise that the cold, heartless Heather wasn't the one for him.

She paused outside the front entrance, manicuring her fingernails with her teeth. She could do this...

'Not as impressive as you'd hoped?' a deep, warm velvet-smooth voice said right behind her.

She curled her toes, closing her eyes and savouring the sensation. There was something innately comforting about having a man standing right behind you, protecting your back, his attention on you, his warm scent surrounding you, his arms so close that he could wrap them around you at any moment.

The idea awakened every nerve in her body to the possibility of being in a man's arms again.

Roxanne swung around. A wall of human body filled the space behind her. Cade Taylor Watson— seriously hunky, seriously sexy and definitely trouble.

He looked damned cute in fawn trousers and a polo shirt and she couldn't help but let her gaze wander higher, from his very nicely shaped chest to his chin, to his sexy mouth and those eyes. Golden eyes that glittered down at her.

'Hello, Roxanne. I'm glad you decided to come.'

'Hi,' she managed, taking several deep breaths to control the surge of emotion coursing traitorously through her. 'You're looking very nice.'

'Thanks.' He slid a hand to the hollow of her back and guided her through the entrance of the gallery. 'I probably should take your number in case something comes up next time.'

'Next time?' she echoed.

'I don't mean I want anything from you by coming here today. I just want to make sure you know that

you're a wonderful person and that somewhere, someone will make you very happy.'

She darted him a look. Had he read her mind? 'I
was going to say the same thing to you.' She tried to
smile but couldn't. Was he sorry for her being alone,
eating alone, being desperate enough to try to pick up
a guy in a club?

She didn't want anyone's pity, least of all his. 'You
should know that there are a lot of wonderful women
out there looking for a guy like you, someone who
would appreciate your smile, your doodling and your
company.'

'Thanks, but I do have Heather, my fiancée.'

'You broke up.'

'I know, but with your help—'

It had been *with* her help! She wanted to yell it.
Gawd, it was as if the man was here just to torture
the truth out of her with his kindness.

'Interesting photo,' she blurted, lunging into the
gallery and over to the framed print on the wall of a
building that looked as if it had been chiselled from
solid rock.

She could feel him behind her, and the urge to step
backwards was overwhelming, and ridiculously stupid.

'I dream of designing a really significant building
like that.' Cade sighed behind her. 'What do you
dream of?'

Roxanne nodded. She could see him building some

incredible building that people would just walk past and gasp at. Is that what the drawings on the napkins were about?

What did she want? 'Castles in the air.'

'Doesn't sound like a safe building site and an absolute nightmare for insuring,' he whispered in her ear.

She swung around to face him. He was right behind her, a hair's breadth from her. She looked up into his gorgeous eyes, her gaze dropping to his mouth. 'Sometimes dreams are all we have.'

Cade's brow furrowed. 'Sometimes you have to put some effort in to make dreams come true.'

She swung back to the picture. 'I would like a family of my own one day, and a kick-arse business of my own and world peace, of course.'

'Hmm,' he murmured behind her. 'Sounds manageable, do-able, and the world peace sounds good too.'

If only it was that easy, but every moment with Cade made it all harder, and more confusing. 'Does Heather enjoy these exhibitions?'

'She says she does,' he murmured behind her.

His breath touched her ear, sending delicious shivers racing down her spine.

'But she doesn't come often. She's busy a lot and I think she prefers her art to be more subjective and a whole lot less realistic.' He moved up beside her. 'But she does have a very enthusiastic attraction to modern sculpture and painting.'

Roxanne wandered to the next print, a photo of a building taken from the ground, looking up to where the top of the building melted into the sky as though it had been constructed to reach the heavens.

Her mind spun. She had to prove to him that Heather was wrong for him! 'That must be hard, not sharing the same interests. I'm sure there'd be plenty of women out there eager to enjoy galleries, intimate dinners, your family, your life with you.'

He shrugged.

'I guess you had long conversations walking hand in hand with Heather, through the park, on the beach, and in the mountains.' She looked ceilingward, closing her eyes, envisaging the woman she'd met with her teetering high heels being an inside person who didn't like to get sand in her shoes, dirt on her hands or bugs in her hair. 'You know, the sort that go on and on all night…where you want to find out everything about the other person.' The sort of long nights you saw in the movies and read about in books.

'Is that what *you* had with your last boyfriend?' he asked, his voice deep and velvet-soft, his gaze on the next print.

She glanced at him. 'My last boyfriend—?'

'The one that broke your—'

She covered her chest. 'How did you—?' He couldn't know about Aaron, could he? He didn't even know her full name.

She looked away, avoiding his golden eyes. There

was no way she could tell him about Aaron, or David or Steve. It was all too painful to consider after what had happened, every time.

He wouldn't look at her the same ever again.

'What was it? He couldn't have cheated on you; you're too smart and witty and beautiful to be looking anywhere else. And he couldn't have ignored you because you're too nice to ignore. And he couldn't have wanted to spend too much time with his mates if he had you waiting for him.'

She looked up at him. Was he hitting on her or was he just the nicest man ever? Oh, gawd, let him be hitting on her…

Her nerves quivered, her eyes stung and she had to look away again. He was just too nice for her own good.

'I'm sorry. I didn't mean to pry,' he murmured, bending down, trying to catch her gaze.

'No, it's not…' she choked, trying to breathe. She wasn't going to cry. He hadn't touched a nerve. It was just because Heather Moreton was stupid, that she had had a nice guy and had thrown him away.

She was just sad for him because he couldn't see that he was better off without that woman in his life.

'He should be shot for hurting you like that.' Cade looked around him, pulled out a handkerchief that looked as if it had never been used, the creases still pressed as cleanly and stiffly as if it had just left the packaging. 'Tell me his name so I can go and give him what he deserves.'

She shook her head, trying to smile. 'It's not what you think.'

'How's that?'

'He didn't break it off,' she whispered. It didn't matter if she told him…she wasn't going to see the man ever again. '*I* did.'

'Oh?'

She could see his mind running through the possible reasons and knew there was no way he could come up with the right one. She couldn't understand it herself, but yet it kept happening.

'I can't say *I do*.'

He faced her, his mouth pulled tight. 'You were considering marrying him?'

Them… She nodded, the memory of the last time, her in her wedding dress… Aaron at the altar in a tuxedo, looking nervous, and he was such a nice guy, had seemed like a wonderful man to have a family with and his family were incredible.

The words had stuck in her throat, visions of what terrors could lie before them consuming her, like what had happened to her parents—the cruel betrayal that their marriage had become and the hurt that had festered, gnawing away at those left behind.

Marriage wasn't for her. She couldn't trust men. She took a deep, slow breath. 'When we got to the church I couldn't… I couldn't marry him.'

After Aaron she had been convinced that she was a hopeless case. Nobody should have to go through that three times. It was as much as she could bear to watch three men walk away because she couldn't trust enough to take the plunge…she deserved to be alone.

A cold wave washed over her. She'd helped Heather do the same thing, had helped her out of her marriage commitment, but just in a less straightforward, honest sort of way.

Why couldn't Heather have just faced the man in her life and told him the truth—that she was scared to death of making a mistake that could ruin both their lives?

She darted a look at Cade from beneath lowered lashes. At least this time she could help the man through the next stage…rather than just being racked with guilt and helplessness.

If she could get the guy to listen to her advice…but maybe she wasn't being clear enough?

Cade's brow was furrowed, his eyes shadowed as though he was looking at her anew.

Oh, gawd. She had just told Cade she was the same as Heather, willing to opt out rather than making a commitment to a guy…

Would he hate her?

'I wouldn't worry about it.' He leant close. 'You'll find the right man for you and when you do you won't have a doubt in the world.'

She couldn't help but look up at him, marvelling at his optimism. 'You think?'

He leant close and brushed his lips over her forehead. 'I know.'

Shock rippled through her.

He'd kissed her! Just like that he'd leant over and planted his hot mouth against her flesh. And it felt awesome…too good.

She shouldn't feel like this.

She wanted to laugh it off, but couldn't.

Cade swung away and took two flutes of champagne off a passing waiter's tray. 'A toast. To understanding the opposite sex, and ourselves,' he proposed, offering her a flute.

Roxanne took the glass carefully. He couldn't just let her confession slide? Not when Heather had done the same thing to him? Not when he'd kissed her as if she mattered. Not when she'd done him the biggest wrong.

Was she just like Heather?

'Understanding?' she bit out, squashing the delight at his warm kiss. 'The only understanding you need about women is that breaking off the romance, whatever the reason, is because of the way *they* feel; whether you think it's logical, rational or sane isn't important.'

'I get that.'

'But you don't get it. She's reconsidered, and she's not going to marry you, she's not going to take the risk, so you have to get on with your life and let her go.'

Cade looked down into her face, his brow creased. He shook his head slowly. 'No, she's been misled, that's all.'

Roxanne stared at the guy. How could he be in such denial…?

He looked past her to somewhere on the other side of the room. 'Hey, I want you to meet someone.'

Roxanne's heart beat faster. Oh, gawd. No. He couldn't have set her up with Heather Moreton, not now.

Why wouldn't he? That was why he'd gone to all the trouble of finding her, that was what he wanted, for her to tell his fiancée that he was a saint and should be treasured.

But how could she tell the truth, and what would Heather say when she saw her, and with her ex of all people…?

Cripes. She'd think something was up, that she'd exaggerated her report to go out with her man.

She gripped the stem of her glass more tightly. A woman like that would sue, without a doubt, and Nadine's business wouldn't survive.

She'd destroy what little hope Nadine had left. And it would all be Roxanne's fault.

Cade swept across the room in front of her and she started to follow, her feet growing heavier with every step.

She couldn't.

There was too much at stake.

She stopped, her heart thundering, turned and rushed towards the door, leaving behind her one chance of helping a guy through the kind of disaster she usually caused.

She strode straight to the kerb and hailed a taxi. There were other ways to find peace with her past— she didn't need him. Besides, there was nothing much else to say.

She'd done what she could.

She just hoped it was enough.

CHAPTER EIGHT

CADE dropped his car keys on to the hall stand. The woman was driving him crazy. She was there one minute pouring out her heart and soul, seeking some sort of understanding on his part for her behaviour with her last boyfriend. And gone the next.

She was obviously haunted by it. He hadn't wanted to push her. She must have needed to let it out and he had been only too willing to let her do so.

She was as mixed up as Heather was at the moment. But he could solve Heather's concerns with him once he got Roxanne to prove that nothing had gone on between them that was inappropriate.

Did he still want to?

Roxanne's words had hit home. His time with Heather hadn't been anything like the intimate long-conversations-well-into-the-night, walk-in-the-park, hold-hands-on-the-beach sort of relationship Roxanne had spoken of.

Was he deluding himself? And Heather?

If only Roxanne hadn't rushed off.

He wrenched off his jacket and flung it over the back of a chair. Did she feel guilty for sharing too much with him, a total stranger, or just embarrassed for getting it all off her chest?

Or was it his damned stupid behaviour that had scared her off. What the hell was he doing, kissing a woman he didn't know…? He hadn't even thought about it. Had just done it. And it had felt amazing.

Should he feel this way about a platonic kiss on the forehead? He wouldn't have thought it possible.

Roxanne would have liked Petra, if she'd stuck around to meet her. His little sister prided herself on her small gallery and the many patrons that visited the exhibitions she arranged.

Getting the gallery up and running had made all the difference to his sister. Putting all her energy into the exhibitions had taken her focus off her personal life and on to her professional one. That had made all the difference. She hadn't been radiating *desperate to date* but a calm assurance. And John had fallen head over heels in love with her. They were going to marry in June.

He shook his head. He had to get the young woman's focus away from what she didn't have and on to what she did have in her life. Her job, her family, her hobbies and her dreams for the future.

Cade couldn't help the surge inside him, an excitement in finding out all about Roxanne.

He kicked off his shoes and strode across to the kitchen, taking a beer from the fridge. Roxanne had bowled him over today. She'd looked amazing…had been amazing…her skin smooth and hot under his lips…dammit.

Roxanne's simple elegance had struck him hard. She hadn't gone all out to look like a model but she'd looked nice, as though she was there to be with him not to show off her latest outfit, shoes, hair, nails…

He shook himself. Heather wasn't like that; she was all warmth and over-the-top sweetness to everyone. He'd never heard her utter a cross word until the other night. *Was that natural?*

That last night with Heather had been a disaster. If he'd suspected what was coming, he could have been ready to defend himself, comfort her, assure her it was all going to be okay, to trust him, that the information had been wrong.

He'd been taken unaware. Like Roxanne was always striking him unaware. Every time he'd underestimated her, and his own reaction.

He cradled the beer in his hands. He couldn't forget the sizzle in his veins at the sweet compliments Roxanne had given him. How she'd been out to emphasise his good points, the opportunities he had, how women would find him attractive.

Cade rubbed his jaw. Why would she say that? And why was he pleased that other women found him attractive? He had Heather, or would do again once he straightened this mess out.

His mind leapt traitorously to Roxanne.

He gulped down half the beer. And it wasn't as if Roxanne was suggesting she included herself in 'women' in general…or that she found him attractive herself.

He closed his eyes and rubbed his jaw. She confused the hell out of him.

Why couldn't it be easy to do the right thing? By everyone?

Heather's pain haunted him. She'd been so hell-bent on this wedding three months ago. Had been thrilled about getting engaged…making the announcements in the paper, the engagement party, the wedding plans.

He'd loved her enthusiasm for them to be together for ever, had loved the way she had embraced his family and encouraged him to spend time with hers. But were they right for each other?

He'd just landed his partnership and had decided he was ready for a long-term relationship and fate had given him Heather.

He'd just turned thirty-two. Prime time to settle down and take a wife. He'd been long enough playing the field, being the bachelor, being carefree. It was time he got serious and Heather had been all for them to have a serious life together.

If only she hadn't got so busy at work. They probably could have done with getting to know each other better. Like he already felt he was getting to know Roxanne.

He walked to the sofa and dropped on to it, leaning

back and closing his eyes, balancing the beer in his hands.

After all the work Heather had put into the wedding it seemed a shame for her to be swayed by some false innuendo.

It was up to him to make it right for her. To get her to understand his sincerity to their future and, most importantly, to vindicate her trust. Like he was trying to impress upon Roxanne—that there was hope.

The poor woman. She needed someone to tell her it was all going to be okay. That it was okay to break it off with a man and leave him at the altar. Far better than marrying him and doing it later.

Cade cringed at the thought of divorce. It was the last thing *he* wanted. He wanted what his parents had. A loving, sharing relationship that spanned thirty-five years.

He loosened his tie. The chances of that were looking a bit slim at the moment…but once he convinced Heather that he was the man she'd said yes to, the same man that she'd enjoyed countless plays and operas with, the same man that she'd declared was the only man for her…it would all be okay again.

Or would it? Did he really want it to be?

The phone rang.

He leant over and picked it up. 'Cade Taylor Watson.'

'Hello, honey, I just wanted to see how you were doing,' his mother chirped. Silence. 'How could you not tell us…we just heard the wedding's off—from Heather's sister. She's ringing around telling everyone.'

Cade raked a hand through his hair. He was sure Heather's sister wouldn't be shy about telling everyone why either. His supposed infidelity was juicy gossip indeed and, unlike Heather, she seemed to enjoy the disasters of others.

'The church rang us to confirm the cancellation and we didn't know what to say. Is everything okay, honey? What happened? Heather and you are the perfect couple. What could have gone wrong?'

Dammit. Cade clenched his fist. He'd hoped he could prove his commitment to Heather before things got this far…and more than anything he'd hoped he could keep this from his parents until it was sorted out.

'She suggested the reason was you,' she paused. 'That you had—'

'I didn't do anything,' he said calmly, imagining the innuendo that Heather's sister would have put on it. She was the epitome of gossip, of titbits and tales. He could imagine her thriving on this.

'Your father and I are behind you one hundred per cent, son,' she said, a tiredness in her voice. 'No matter what.'

Cade felt the words like a punch in his guts. Hell. His father was a solicitor, his mother a teacher; the last thing they would want to hear was that their guidance on honesty and integrity over the years had been ignored by their only son for the cheap thrill of bedding down with the woman in red.

He took a hurried gulp of the beer.

'Thanks,' he said quickly. 'But there's not a problem. Heather has just been misguided by some arrant gossip that is entirely untrue.'

'I know how much this wedding means to you both, and goodness, then there's your reputation to consider…your father and I don't want everyone thinking you're some—'

'No, I don't either.'

'So I expect you've been over there talking with Heather about this?'

Cade's mind froze. He hadn't. It hadn't even occurred to him. Why not?

Surely any sensible man interested in working it out would have chased after his fiancée to convince her of his love. And what had he done?

All he'd thought about was finding Roxanne.

Maybe his priorities were askew. Maybe he needed to have a good hard think about his engagement, about his feelings for Heather and what he really wanted.

He had to put things in perspective. One thing he did know, no matter what, was that he couldn't have Heather or his family thinking he was a cheat.

He had to find the woman in red again, and this time solve her problems before thinking of his.

His could wait.

All he had to do was help Roxanne, then get her to tell her side of his story to Heather and clear his name.

But how in hell was he going to find her?

Roxanne picked up the last cup, rubbing the surface dry with the tea towel as she balanced against the bench, her foot massaging the underbelly of the Scottish terrier at her feet.

Pumpkin wagged his tail against the linoleum. Rory had named the shameless pup Pumpkin after her favourite fairy tale and what he could turn into given a bit of magic and a fairy godmother.

The house was an antique, situated an easy distance from the city centre. It was as narrow as the office, but stretched deep with high ceilings giving the illusion of space.

A hallway ran down one side, the entire length of the house, with the rooms branching from it. The lounge room was first, then the two bedrooms and then the kitchen and dining room and a small bathroom-cum-laundry at the rear.

It was small, cosy and a bit cramped but Nadine had warmed the place with a bit of paint, colonial furniture and knick-knacks and Rory had spread her little touch of disaster to make it a home.

The floral sofa was scattered with cushions and soft toys, with a coffee table in front of it, a stack of magazines, colouring books and picture books littered across the surface. Soft pink curtains hung at the narrow windows that looked out to the neighbouring building's western wall and the little walkway that ran down the side of the house to the backyard that was just big enough to swing a teddy in.

She looked over to her sister and Rory, who were sitting at the small round dining table, the weight of her secret lying in the pit of her stomach like lead.

She had to tell her.

Sure, it had been over two weeks now since her last encounter with Cade and the risk had to have reduced. The chance of Heather Moreton storming into Nadine's office now and throwing accusations around about her unprofessional behaviour was minimal, but she had to get rid of her burden.

She felt as if she was sinking deeper and deeper into something she had no control over.

She touched her forehead. Cade haunted her.

Maybe if she told her sister what had happened while she was out of the office she could stop thinking about Cade, of his deep voice, of his golden eyes and his kindness to her.

She'd heave this weight off her chest and be free to think of other things, and feel a whole lot less for the guy.

Besides, Nadine had to know the truth so she could sleep at night. She needed to know that Nadine was armed and ready if something went wrong. She had to know that she had messed up again and she needed her help to assuage her guilt.

Her sister leaned closer to her daughter, a healthy colour now since the flu had passed. She looked a lot like them both, with brown hair with natural auburn highlights, green eyes and olive skin.

Rory was nearly five years old, fresh from the bath, squeaky clean, her hair still wet, and in pyjamas that were covered in small rabbits.

Just looking at her niece stirred Roxanne's innards in the vicinity of her biological clock that she could hear clunking loudly.

She twisted the tea towel. She could let Nadine think everything was okay and it probably was—the potential for a disaster to happen upon her business was getting slimmer by the minute—but she sure could use her help to get her over this fixation on Cade.

Roxanne hung the tea towel on the oven door and wiped her hands dry on her jeans. 'Nadine,' she ventured, testing the water.

Nadine tied off the end of Rory's plait. 'Go jump into bed; I'll be there in a minute.'

Roxanne wandered closer to her sister, who was packing up the game on the table, breathing deep and slow, trying to muster the courage for this. 'I need to ask your advice.'

'If this is about a man, forget it.' She stabbed the dice towards Roxanne. 'You know my track record, you know your track record, you know our parents' track record.'

Roxanne crossed her arms over her chest. 'What are you implying?'

'We're hopeless. I'm a disillusioned romantic, our parents died alone and lonely, and you, my dear sister, are in denial.'

'About what?' Maybe she should have read Nadine's horoscope for the day before venturing into territory that she couldn't help but lecture her endlessly about. The bane of having a pessimistic Scorpio sister with a serious sermon complex.

Roxanne threw up her hands, warding off the speech that was doubtlessly coming. Since their mother's death nine years ago it was as though Nadine had taken on the role with a vengeance. She was forever telling her what she should do and, more often, what she shouldn't.

'I'm perfectly okay,' Roxanne begged, holding her crossed fingers behind her. 'So kindly don't you lump me in with you lot.'

'Let me see.' Nadine put up her hand and folded down her thumb. 'There's Kevin, who left you because you wouldn't talk to him.'

'Kevin was too needy.'

She folded down another finger. 'There's David, who left you because you wouldn't give him an answer to his proposal.'

'I was thinking.'

Nadine raised her eyebrows. 'There's Steve, who

you broke up with a month after you accepted his proposal.'

'I made a mistake saying yes.'

'And then there's Aaron, who you left standing at the altar with a dazed expression on his face because you'd dashed off before the I dos.' She dropped her hand and folded the game board.

Roxanne bit her bottom lip. 'There's a perfectly good reason for that. All that.'

'Yes.' Her sister put the board and pieces into the box. 'You're afraid to commit.'

'I am not.' She didn't have any trouble committing. She'd been in heaps of relationships, just not the right one, with the right guy, at the right time.

'Fine, whatever.' Nadine sighed deeply. 'So what's your question about?'

Roxanne dropped into a seat at the table, looking up at her sister. 'Work.'

Nadine rolled her eyes. 'Thank God for that, but I don't want to talk about work now. The books are a nightmare. Things are a bit tight... I shouldn't have taken a week off—we could've done with me doing more work and passing less on.'

'Yes.' Roxanne cringed. So much for coming clean...there was no way. Not now. Nadine had enough to worry about, besides it *was* over. There'd be no way Cade could find her again. She wasn't going to go to that restaurant again or the bar...they were safe. And the likelihood of Heather storming into the office… Roxanne didn't want to think about it. 'I'm going to look for something else now that I've got your office in order.'

'It's been great.' Nadine snapped the lid on the box and returned it to the cupboard in the living area. 'Do you have to?'

She swallowed her confession. 'You're not bringing in enough to feed me as well. Besides, I like challenges.'

'Me too, and just now my challenge is to get my little girl into her bed and read her a story, unless you want to?'

'Will the story be about princes and princesses and happy ever afters?' she asked, quashing the turmoil deep in her belly.

'Yep. The stuff that only happens in fairy tales.' Nadine stared towards the window as though she was a million miles away.

Roxanne looked away. Was she thinking about what her and her hubby had had together? What she'd lost? What she'd missed out on by marrying the jerk so young or what could be waiting for her in the future?

'Okay.' She strode to Rory's door. It was probably better Nadine didn't know what a drop-kick she'd been anyway. She wouldn't want to hear what a risk she'd taken with the business by saving a nice man from a fate called Heather.

Nadine was wrong. She didn't have any trouble

with men…just one man in particular who wanted something from her that she couldn't give.

She shook her head.

It didn't matter now. She'd never see the guy again… There was no way he could find her…she'd left him no clues, had made sure of it.

She'd never see Cade again.

Dark, cold emptiness washed over her and her throat ached. Stupid, because she hardly knew the guy…

It was time to put the past behind her and get on with life… She wouldn't have to think about Cade ever again.

CHAPTER NINE

'ARE you expecting a delivery?'

Roxanne dragged on her grey track suit top, leaving the zip open, quite liking the effect of the apricot tank top underneath contrasting with the seriously cute grey jogging outfit she'd picked up on sale.

It hugged her shape just enough to show she was female, wasn't too baggy and had a bit of style. She pulled on her trainers, tying the laces quickly.

She loved mail. Probably because she didn't get a lot. As a kid she'd check the mailbox every day in the hope of mail from her dad, but it had never come.

Delivery? She'd been successful bidding on a vase and a CD on Ebay, but she'd only paid yesterday…that was quick.

She stared at the incredible invention for surfing the Net in the corner of the bedroom. It had been Nadine's room but she'd given it up for her to sleep in while she bunked with Rory.

Roxanne was thankful for her sacrifice. The computer was perfect for consuming large chunks of time, sparing her from thinking about a certain male.

She shook her head. She had to get on with her own future and leave her sister's—find a place of her

own, a job of her own, a life of her own again. And
she knew the only way *not* to muck it up again was
to stay alone.

She stood up, donning her cap, pulling it low over
the shadows under her eyes, a vague sort of emptiness
haunting her chest.

'Yes, I guess I am expecting a delivery,' she called
back to her sister. 'Be there in a sec… Where's it
from?'

'He needs your signature.' A pause. 'It's from some
gallery.'

Yes. It was the print she'd bought. The one that
they'd stared at together, the building that soared into
the heavens…the one that reminded her of him. The
one she could imagine him designing…while he was
dreaming of great things, a great future with Heather,
that was all an illusion.

She stared at the bedroom door. She shouldn't have
gone back to the gallery—it was too high a risk—but
she wanted something to remind her of him, something more than a stilted photo of the guy wrapped
around Heather Moreton.

She glanced over to the book on the bedside table.
So, the photo of him hadn't made it back into the
file…it didn't mean anything.

She tore her attention from *How to be a Stud* and
yanked open the bedroom door, stepping into the hallway, passing Nadine shuffling back to the kitchen in

her dressing gown and fluffy slippers, her hair ruffled by sleep.

The television was on in the front room, the shrieks and high voices suggesting cartoons.

Roxanne moved towards the front door, her attention drawn to the delivery man filling the doorway. She couldn't look away.

Her chest tightened.

She saw the small flat parcel in his hands, wrapped in brown paper, trying to quash the silly reaction. It was just a picture.

The lady at the gallery hadn't let her take it away until the exhibition was over…she'd only waited two weeks but it had felt like an eternity.

She held out her hands, her stomach a mass of tangled nerves, her mind trying to suppress the irrational response. It was only a picture of a building.

The delivery guy just stood there.

Roxanne slowly took the guy in, the blue jeans, the sweatshirt, the baseball cap pulled low over…a face that she thought she'd never see again.

'Cade?' she breathed.

'Hi.'

A delicious warmth spread through her body at his deep smooth voice. 'What are you doing here?'

He leant against the doorframe, his shoulders and chest perfectly outlined in the tight shirt. 'I work part-time at the gallery delivering prints around the city on Saturday mornings to women that run off and don't even leave a glass slipper behind for the poor old prince to find her again.'

Roxanne's vision blurred. Oh, gawd. He'd found her. Again.

It wasn't over…

Cade handed her the package. 'Your print. Good choice, by the way.'

She nodded, her brain stalling. She took the picture and gripped it tightly to her. Oh, gawd. Oh, jeez. Oh, cripes. What in heavens was she going to say? Do? She sucked in a quick breath. 'How?'

His mouth quirked and his golden eyes bathed her in warmth. 'Well, if the clock hadn't struck midnight at the gallery for you, you would have met the owner, my sister.'

'Sister,' she gasped, the words slicing through what was left of her control. What an idiot she was…it hadn't been Heather he had wanted her to meet, it had been his sister!

She could have stayed with him longer…stolen a few more moments of a dream that couldn't be.

No. She'd done the right thing…it was better she'd escaped and ended it. She'd said all she wanted to anyway. There was nothing more she could do.

He pulled a pen out of his back pocket and twirled it around in his hand. 'Now, Cinderella, since you didn't leave a shoe I can't offer you anything but…'

'She's not Cinderella,' Rory said, poking her head out of the lounge room.

Cade glanced down at Rory and jerked his gaze back to Roxanne, his eyes wide.

Roxanne could read the question but was loath to answer. It would be so easy to scare him away with a child…wouldn't it? *If* Rory had been hers…better that than having to face another goodbye.

Cade squatted down to Rory. 'Well, hello there. Who are you?'

'Rory.' She wore teddy pyjamas, her hair sticking out at all angles, the dusty flush of sleep on her cheeks, her eyes too bright.

He looked back up at Roxanne. 'And which one of the beautiful ladies that live here is your mother? Cinderella or Sleeping Beauty?'

A gurgle of laughter erupted from Rory. 'Mummy isn't sleeping,' she said, thrusting her finger down the hallway. 'She's in the kitchen.'

'Then this beautiful lady is—?'

'Aunty Rox.' Rory grinned, putting her hands on her hips and staring into Cade's face. 'You can have *her.*'

Cade glanced back at her, a smile pulling at the corners of his mouth. 'Really?'

Roxanne opened her mouth but no words would come. Her stomach was invaded by butterflies, swarming upwards to her chest, making it hard to breathe, talk, even think.

How embarrassing. Given away by your niece…

what would he think of Rory not wanting her to stay with them?

What did she care? This was over. So over. Why was he even here…to torture her some more?

Roxanne looked at Cade's large body filling the doorway, every nerve ignited by his powerful presence. And he was definitely here…she couldn't escape this time.

Rory leant close. 'Her slippers are upstairs. If you want me to…I can get one for you.'

Cade stood up, a deep rumble emanating from inside him. 'Slipper?'

Rory nodded enthusiastically. 'To slip on her foot so you know she's the one.'

Roxanne looked to the ceiling, praying for help. This couldn't get any worse…

Cade ruffled Rory's hair, beaming down at the little girl with warm eyes and an even warmer smile. 'That's okay. I think I can manage without one.'

Rory nodded, folding her arms over her chest. 'Go on then.'

Cade lifted his gaze to face Roxanne.

Oh, gawd. She liked it better when he was being wonderful and sweet to Rory, his attention on Rory, not her.

Cade settled on his knees in front of her.

She couldn't believe this was happening. It shouldn't be. The risk should have been over…but then, maybe he'd changed his mind about Heather, maybe it wasn't about getting his fiancée back any more, maybe it was about her...

Warmth flowed through her. *Her*? The perfect guy was here to see her? Had she touched him and he couldn't get her out of his mind?

Could she do this?

Cade glanced at Rory, then back to her, his gaze slowly moving from her trainers, up her grey track pants up and over her apricot top, clinging to her breasts giving everything away.

Rory touched Cade's sleeve. 'She usually looks better.'

He nodded, clasping his hands in front of him. 'I'll keep that in mind.'

Roxanne stared down at him on his knees, the roar of her blood thundering in her ears, her cheeks heating with fire and her mind scrambling for her to withdraw to somewhere safe.

What was he doing?

The grin on Rory's face widened. 'Good, keep going. You can do it.'

Roxanne drew her attention back to Cade, to his deep golden eyes, to his mouth, that promised so much, that she couldn't start to consider. Not until she knew what he was doing here...not until she had guarantees.

'Will you, Roxanne,' he said, his deep voice washing over her, 'do me the honour of accompanying me on a walk?'

She let out the breath she'd been holding, losing several inches in confidence. That was it? This Romeo act was obviously just for Rory's benefit then... nothing more.

Rory stepped forward. 'That's it? Aren't you going to ask her to marry you?'

Roxanne wished for a giant hole to swallow her up.

The corners of Cade's mouth tilted. 'That's awfully fast. Shouldn't I get to know her a bit first?' He leant a little towards Rory. 'I may not like her that much.'

'You're probably right.' Rory nodded slowly as though contemplating his perspective. 'But you will like her.'

'Will I?' He laughed.

Rory nodded again enthusiastically.

Roxanne held her breath, gripping the doorknob in her right hand as though it was a lifeline, praying Rory stopped there and didn't embarrass her any more than she already had. She didn't want to stand in the doorway, she didn't want a walk, she didn't want to deal with this again.

She'd suffered enough these last couple of weeks without another inning with Cade, or the traitorous responses rumbling deep inside her.

Time hadn't changed anything.

'Yes, she's awfully nice.' Rory shot Roxanne a smile. 'She colours with me, reads stories and plays dolls, but she's messed up.'

'Oh?' Cade lifted an eyebrow, casting Roxanne a mischievous grin.

Roxanne dragged in a quick breath. Whatever Rory had picked up lately…she didn't want to find out. She opened her mouth, lifting a hand to stop her. 'Rory—'

'She won't be your princess,' Rory said sadly, resting her hand on Cade's shoulder. 'She can love you, but she won't marry you. Her heart isn't as strong and brave as Mummy's.'

'Oh?' Cade murmured, his voice deep and husky. 'Why?'

'She knows when her prince leaves she'll die of a broken heart,' Rory said. 'Just like *her* mummy did.'

CHAPTER TEN

CADE walked beside Roxanne, his whole body tense. All he wanted to do was pull her into his arms and hold her, tell her it would all be okay. But would it?

Was little Rory right? Was Roxanne walking around keeping the men in her life at arm's length so her heart would be safe?

He glanced around him. The street was quiet for a Saturday morning, the narrow road lined with parked cars…probably everyone having a sleep-in while their kids watched the cartoons on the box.

Like Rory. Hell, the first moment he'd seen her he'd been sure she was Roxanne's. The same eyes, the same colour hair and the same richly tanned skin. If he hadn't seen her mother first, Roxanne's sister, he probably would have made a fool of himself.

That would *not* have been great. Complimenting Roxanne on her beautiful little girl…

He could imagine her children looking just like that cute little angel… It sounded as if she'd make the perfect mother. Rory certainly liked her, despite her enthusiasm to give her to him.

Cade shook himself.

He shouldn't be thinking about Roxanne in that

way...should he? Hell, he probably shouldn't have gone down on one knee in front of her. But it had felt incredible, like the fantasy that Rory thought it was. Nothing like when he had proposed to Heather. And he had only been proposing a walk!

How could that be?

He pulled back his shoulders and threw out his chest. It was nothing. Nothing compared to the wonderful future he and Heather had planned in great detail...and should be working actively at getting back.

This...with Roxanne...this feeling...was something he couldn't gauge, he couldn't rely on...and he wasn't going to accept.

He hadn't been brought up that way. If you could see it, analyse it, categorise it, it was real. It had served him well, in business, with his mates and with Heather.

Roxanne kept pace beside him, her body hidden under the track suit, giving him only tantalising glimpses of the curves he knew were beneath. Her hips were obvious, and the length of her legs, and the open jacket revealed the exquisite shape of her breasts. She'd make some guy really happy...

Rory's words spun in his head, torturing him. Was there any truth to it, or was it a culmination of too much television, fairy tales and overheard snippets of adult conversation?

Or was it how she said?

He hoped not. It would be damned hard to solve

her problems if that was the case. Not just a matter of boosting a woman's confidence but a total overhaul on her perceptions of men. He'd have his work cut out for him.

From the mouth of babes? Were Roxanne *and* Rory's mother doomed to failed relationships because of their parents' failed marriage?

'Where's Rory's dad?' he asked, glancing at the woman beside him, wary of getting too personal with the questions too soon.

'He's around,' she said tightly. 'They were divorced six months ago and they're taking it hard.'

Cade slipped his hands into his jeans pockets. 'What was it? Irreconcilable differences?'

'Irresistible Deidre,' she said, faltering. 'Secretary and home-wrecker.'

He stopped and turned to her. 'And they couldn't work it out?'

Roxanne stared at the ground, nibbling her bottom lip. 'My sister felt another woman in the marriage was a bit of a crowd.'

'He wouldn't give Deidre up?' he asked carefully.

Roxanne shook her head, a shadow passing over her face. 'No, and still hasn't.'

He couldn't imagine what it would be like to be cast aside like that. 'I'm sorry.'

'Me too.' She looked up at him, her sea-green eyes flashing. 'My sister is a really nice person, if a bit bossy at times…and Rory's a doll.'

He swallowed hard. 'She's a sweet kid but getting the wrong idea about love and marriage.'

She shrugged, stepping out again. 'I guess.'

He followed and caught her hand, wrapping it in his. He couldn't think that Rory was right about Roxanne, about her sister...

He hadn't felt like this since high school. He didn't know what to say or do to make her feel better about herself...about her future.

Her small fingers flexed around the edge of his hand, her thumb nestled under his, their wrists brushing as they walked. He could almost feel the beat of her pulse.

Silence slid between them.

The more he found out, the more he wanted to help, and the more he was driven to.

They approached a park, bathed in the strong spring sunshine, with kids playing on the playground and neat houses facing the area. But it was all secondary to that touch, where flesh met, where her heat and his mingled, intoxicating him.

Visions of her in that red dress. That time at the restaurant surged unbidden to him...and the next time, the conversation over cannelloni, her sweet voice, the scent of vanilla, her sparkling green eyes and that mouth, full red lips...of brushing his lips over her sweet skin...

She *was* a prize, for someone else.

They turned the corner again, back on to her street.

He was running out of time. Say something, you idiot. Anything.

'I like the outfit,' he blurted, cringing at his idiocy. He should have gone with the surroundings, the architecture, the weather...his mind darted back to their first meeting again—unforgettable.

'This,' she said, slipping her hand out of his and swinging her arms wide, a smile pulling at her full lips. 'Not exactly Cinderella.'

'Do you believe in fairy tales?'

'No, of course not.' She glanced at him, pulled the corners of her jacket together and crossed her arms over her chest.

'Why not? Don't you deserve a handsome prince?' Like his sister had figured she deserved one. Like his mother had. Like Rory thought she did. 'A happy ever after?'

'Of course I deserve one,' she lilted. 'But I'm not silly enough to believe all that.'

He couldn't argue with that one. He cleared his throat. 'There may not be princes out there but there'll be a nice man for you somewhere who will love you as much as you deserve.'

She shook her head. 'Finding a partner to share your life with is just chance. Luck.'

'And how's your luck?'

She smiled at him. 'Pitiful.'

His gut ached at the thought of her giving up. After she'd been so optimistic with him that night at the bar and then at the same restaurant… Was it his fault? He hoped not.

Was the little girl right? Had she given up? Was she doomed? Did *she* think she was doomed?

'Tell me about your mother,' he blurted.

'Not much to tell.' She looked away. 'My dad left her when I was a child. She was sad, cried all the time, and then she got sick.'

'And died.'

'Yes.'

'Of a broken heart?' he asked carefully, watching her as she pushed open the small gate at the front of her place.

Roxanne turned on the doorstep and stared up into his face with her emerald-green eyes. 'Well, that's what love's all about, isn't it?'

He shook his head. 'No. It's about—'

'What? Soul-swapping sessions? Intimate walks sharing dreams and goals?' She pursed her lips tight, her eyes flashing. 'Great sex? Someone that you care for more than you care for yourself? Having that someone to share your life with? Have babies with?'

'All that,' he said slowly, her words hitting home again. Had he had any of that with Heather?

They had pleasant outings. They had a good friendship. She had been warm and sweet to everyone and everyone had liked her, but had it gone deeper? That deep?

Cade swallowed hard, the realisation seeping into

him. *What sort of idiot was he?* He had had nothing of the kind with Heather!

He'd analysed the form of love that he'd seen in his parents' relationship and his friends' and had sketched out a two-dimensional representation of it and had gone out and found it.

Where was the rest? All those things Roxanne had said…all those things that were usually hidden from outsiders' eyes? Not with Heather… Would it come later, after some time? Or did it have to be there from the start, pulsing underneath everything that was said and done?

He was a fool.

Hell, he'd never even looked for them with her. They had kept such a reserved distance from each other, making all the motions, the right noises, to be in love.

But was it love?

Did he even know love?

He raked his hands through his hair. He'd nearly made the biggest mistake of his life.

He sighed deeply. Heather. She had probably felt that there was something missing, that he wasn't giving her everything… Probably why she'd jumped to conclusions when the report of his supposed indiscretion had come in from her family member. She had known something wasn't right, but instead of being in denial, like him, she had found something to support her doubts, however erroneous.

His gut tightened. He still had to make things right for her. He couldn't have her thinking she was anything less than wonderful. He couldn't have her thinking he'd been unfaithful to her, for any reason. And he couldn't have her thinking, like Roxanne did, that trusting a man again, loving a man, was going to hurt her.

Not a chance.

He stared down into Roxanne's sea-green eyes, the need to wipe that pain from her eyes almost as intense as the desire to hold her, close, tight...for ever?

Cade stepped back. This burning desire to find Roxanne wasn't simply for Heather's sake, it was for *his*!

How honest was he?

Was *this* love?

He couldn't help but move closer, letting the feeling seep through him, engulf him in a delicious warmth that radiated from his chest, sparking from the incredibly beautiful woman in front of him.

'Love is having someone that I want to grow old with, someone that I want to die loving me,' he said carefully.

'Cade,' she whispered.

His name on her lips reverberated through him like primitive drums, pounding a message deep into his body.

Love?

He moved even closer to her, reaching out and

touching her cheek with his thumb, slipping his fingers around the back of her neck, under her silken hair, ignoring everything but the throb of desire burning hot in his veins. 'You know what I want?'

He wanted to find out if this was it.

'I think I do.' She bit her lip, staring at her feet. 'But it's not a good idea.'

He lifted her chin with his finger, his mind teasing him with visions of a future with Roxanne, of her lying beside him in bed, of quiet walks, intimate dinners, of the children they could make together…like that little Rory girl. 'I'll do anything to get it.'

The first chance at something special in his life, and he'd nearly missed it because he was a blind fool.

She stared up at him, her eyes wide. 'I'm starting to get that impression.'

'Good.' He drew his finger down her cheek, tracing the soft line of her face, the skin silky smooth under his touch. They couldn't ignore this chance, this magic that sparked between them.

His blood heated.

He drew her closer, leaning down, his gaze on those lips that begged to be kissed.

Gawd, she was incredible. From that first pick-up line he'd wondered what it would be like to be free to taste her lips…had pushed down the desire, the signals that he was attracted to the woman.

It hadn't been appropriate… Now, everything was different.

He hadn't been honest at all. With Heather or himself. And it was time to get honest, because he couldn't deny this...

Roxanne froze. What was he doing?

She couldn't help but look at his sexy mouth and the way it was descending towards hers, couldn't help but glance into his golden-flecked eyes and see the intent blazing there, couldn't help but hold her breath in sweet anticipation.

She closed her eyes. This couldn't be happening, not when he'd just announced he'd do anything to get her to talk to Heather. Was this the 'anything'?

Would it hurt to indulge in this?

His lips brushed hers, cruelly gentle, almost a whisper on the wind, a promise that made her eyes sting and her lips quiver, sending tingles of sensation coursing down her spine.

Where had he been all her life?

His mouth closed over hers, plying her lips with a gentle mastery; an ache ripped through her belly, going deep.

She couldn't help but move her lips beneath his, tasting the sweet dance between them, exploring the inner softness he offered and the wild sensations sizzling through every nerve in her body.

His arms slid around her, holding her close to his hard chest.

His strength filled her, the innate power in him crashing through what little reserve she had left.

She wanted him, wanted Cade's arms around her, wanted his lips, his touch, everything.

Roxanne melted against him, slipping her arms around his waist, parting her lips, surrendering to him and the burning desire pumping through her veins calling his name.

He deepened the kiss, drawing her deep into a passion that she'd never felt before, something almost primal in need.

Cade skimmed his hands up her waist, tracing her curves agonisingly slowly, as though he was memorising her, his thumbs brushing the edge of her breasts, making her itch for the touch of his bare skin against hers, his lips against her flesh, flesh against flesh.

She placed one palm on his chest, the thin fabric doing little to smother the throb of his heart against his ribs.

She pulled back, guilt, solid and icy, crashing into the deep attraction she had for him. 'Cade,' she whispered, looking up into his eyes, the truth poised on the tip of her tongue.

She had to tell him.

He deserved the truth. It was unfair to let him feel…when it was based on a lie…and she knew that lies were no place to start a relationship. Not if you wanted to keep it, and she did.

She wanted to keep him.

Did his heart beat for her or another? Was he just confused, his ego looking for some Band-Aid, and she was it?

Typical. No matter what she did with a guy it was always the same—another mess, another disaster.

How could she escape the fact? She was doomed. No matter what happened, what she did or said, it couldn't change the cold, hard truth.

His heart could never be hers.

CHAPTER ELEVEN

'WHAT—' the voice ripped through the tense silence '—in hell is going on?'

Roxanne took a sharp breath and yanked her hand from Cade's chest.

Nadine stood in the doorway, Rory by her side, both dressed. 'Who the hell are you?'

'That's Prince Charming and that is Cinderella,' Rory offered, pointing at them. 'She wasn't in a dress, but he didn't mind.'

Nadine frowned. 'What?'

Rory stepped forward, stabbing her little finger to Roxanne. 'Mummy, you know Aunty Rox and that—' she swung her finger to Cade '—is the prince that's going to try to save her.'

'From what?' Nadine said, her voice high.

Rory shrugged. 'I don't know.'

Roxanne stepped forward, her cheeks heating annoyingly as though she had been caught on the doorstep by her mother. 'Nadine, this is Cade Taylor Watson. Cade, my sister.'

'He's the delivery guy,' she barked, pushing back her hair, running her eyes over him as though he was an alien.

Roxanne sighed. 'Yes. He's the delivery guy.' But he was so much more…and she didn't know where to start in explaining this. She didn't know quite what had happened or what to do about it herself.

'You picked up the delivery guy?' Nadine yanked Roxanne's sleeve and pulled her towards her. 'Are you that desperate?'

'Nadine.' She felt a fresh rush of embarrassment flooding her cheeks. Leave it to her sister to make things worse.

'Sure, he's cute and all, but hell, girl.' Nadine shooed Rory inside, not taking her eyes off the man towering beside them. 'You're asking for trouble.'

'Nadine, nice to meet you,' Cade offered, holding out his hand in a gesture of peace. 'I know you want the best for your sister, and want to protect her from any more hurt. So do I.'

Roxanne stared at him. He did? She tipped her head. He probably did. He had been all for helping her out from the moment she had met the guy, but where did kissing her help anything?

'Right. *You* just met her,' her sister scoffed, pulling the door closed behind her, probably to protect Rory from hearing them.

'Actually we met several weeks ago,' Roxanne blurted, turning slightly to her sister and glaring at her to be quiet, but that was akin to asking a bee to stop buzzing.

'That would be about the time Rory was sick, yes?

I was pretty flat out then.' She glanced at Roxanne, her brow shadowed. 'I didn't notice you going out, except for work.'

'It wasn't at work.' Cade slipped his hands into his jeans pockets and shrugged. 'What work *do* you do?'

Roxanne's heart leapt into her throat. 'That doesn't matter…right now all that matters is getting Rory some milk and cookies.' She stepped towards the door. 'I'll see you…some time, later.'

She turned the front doorknob and pushed Nadine back into the house, her pulse racing. Oh, gawd. Let her sister shut up. Let her not say another word.

She couldn't have Cade finding out the truth about what they did. What she did. What his beloved Heather had done to him.

Roxanne grabbed the door, starting to close it on the hunk standing wide-eyed on the doorstep, looking as lost as she was feeling by the kiss, her sister, this conversation that was leading where she couldn't possibly let it go. For anyone.

Cade stepped forward. 'Can I see you tonight?

'I—' Her mind tossed. This was so hard. How could she possibly do this, knowing she wasn't his…that the kiss—she touched her still-tingling lips—had been a mistake that he was going to regret.

Or worse…that she was his rebound girl, who he needed to build his confidence to get over the witch, Heather…

No. He wasn't like that.

'I'll make you dinner, something nice.' He shrugged sheepishly, looking down at her with those sexy eyes of his. 'And we can talk.'

Talk. They needed to do that about as much as she needed to step out and fall into his arms again, taste his lips again, feel that amazing oneness one more time before she ended the one thing that felt real in her life.

She gripped the timber door tightly, holding back the urge. 'Sure,' she whispered, not trusting her voice.

He smiled warmly at her, handing her a business card with the name of his company on the front. 'My address is on the back. Eight?'

'Okay.' She backed into the house and closed the door on the most handsome and kindest man she'd ever met, ever kissed. The man who was the closest to Prince Charming as a man could get.

She sagged against the door, struggling with the twist in events that had him on her doorstep. Was he still after that confession to Heather that nothing had happened—or something else?

She touched her lips. Those feelings couldn't be nothing, but could she trust herself this time? Could she trust him?

Roxanne closed her eyes and relived the amazing minutes she'd been wrapped in his strong arms, held by his warm hands, kissed with his hot lips…

She had to get over her problem with men. She

couldn't miss out on this opportunity with Cade, no matter how long it lasted.

She bit her bottom lip. And how long could it last if she told him the truth?

The card was snatched from her hand.

She looked down.

Rory was squinting at the card. 'Is this where his palace is?'

'What?' Nadine stood, arms crossed, in the hallway. Her slight frame, clad in faded blue jeans and a sweat-shirt, belied the intensity of her presence. She was not a happy woman.

Rory threw the card into the air and clapped her hands. 'Aunty Rox is going to the ball, aren't you? Should I get your slippers?'

'Not just now.' Roxanne watched the card flutter to the floor, glancing at her older sister warily. She sucked in a deep breath. 'It might be a good idea to go and play dolls, Rory. Your mummy and I need to talk.'

'Okay.' Rory skipped up the hallway.

Roxanne turned to her older sister, steeling herself for the interrogation that was undoubtedly coming. Since her husband's betrayal Nadine was doubly wary of Roxanne's love life…or, thankfully, as far as her sister was concerned, lack of.

'What is going on?' Nadine put her hands on her hips, glaring at her, her brow furrowed. 'How did you have time to meet him if you were at work…? *Did you meet him at work? Our work? My work?*'

'Nadine.' Roxanne stepped into the lounge room and moved to the sofa, pushing a teddy and two books out of the way and sitting down.

'It's that routine business that brought in that nice fat cheque, isn't it? The one that you don't want to talk about?'

Roxanne stared at her hands. 'Yes, that would be it.'

Nadine waved her hand as though rolling the air in front of her. 'Spill.'

Roxanne took a deep, slow breath, pushing down the rolling waves of fear in her belly. 'I was paid by his fiancée to find out if he'd be unfaithful to her.'

Her sister rolled her eyes. 'Obviously she was right.'

She couldn't meet her sister's gaze. 'Well, yes and no.'

Nadine crossed her arms. 'What do you mean, yes and no? He either was, or wasn't, unfaithful. We're not in the business of vagaries. Did he make an advance on you, or not?'

Roxanne straightened the books and magazines on the coffee table. 'The woman was a real witch.'

Nadine dropped on to the arm of one of the armchairs. 'You did get the advance he made on tape and show the client her fiancé having every intention of being unfaithful?'

She shrugged. 'I didn't want to damage the camera.'

'Tell me you got evidence,' Nadine said softly, leaning forward, her face stricken.

Roxanne's throat burned. She could see that her sister's future in business was racing before her eyes. 'I had a tape recorder—' she jerked to her feet '—and although he didn't exactly proposition me she was keen to go with the idea that there was a lot of touching and innuendo going on.'

'What?'

Roxanne strode to the front window. 'And now he wants me to go and see his fiancée and tell her that he was innocent.' She paused, considering whether he still wanted that or possibly, now, he wanted her.

'But he wasn't, right?' her sister said tightly.

'Well…' Roxanne couldn't face her sister, the magnitude of what she'd put at risk by her exaggeration hitting her harder than ever.

'He did hit on you? Didn't he?' Nadine's voice rose in pitch. 'Please tell me he did and he's just after a white lie to patch up his engagement because he had no idea who you were.'

Roxanne looked at the ceiling. She needed help, needed a distraction, and needed that great black hole to swallow her up so she didn't have to face the disappointment in her sister's eyes.

Nothing came to her…it was time to finally face the music. She turned to her sister. 'No, he didn't hit on me.'

Nadine screwed up her face, her cheeks flushing a deep crimson. 'But…he's with you…and that thing with the lips and the hands on the doorstep isn't exactly being faithful to the woman.'

Roxanne shook her head. 'No. But that's my fault. He thinks I'm in need of male attention and comfort.'

'You are!'

'No.' Roxanne placed her hands in front of her. 'You know, to boost my confidence and get me dating again because as far as he's concerned I've been hurt by a past boyfriend and—'

'You *have* been hurt,' Nadine stated, shaking her head and looking at her as though she was mad. 'And you are dating—*you* just accepted a *date* with *him*.'

Roxanne walked back to the sofa and dropped on to the cushions. 'He's just being nice.'

'You're being blind and stupid.' Nadine stalked towards her. 'I can't believe you've been so stupid. How could you have lied to a client? And without evidence? And now when he comes after you, you think he's nice? Wake up and smell the sweat socks! You can't believe anything a man says or does.'

Roxanne shook her head. 'I'm going to tell him the truth about what actually happened tomorrow.'

'What truth?' Nadine asked, her voice shrill.

'That I embellished the facts to his fiancée because she wanted to believe the worst of him.' Then Cade would be free of Heather, free to explore this amazing chemistry they had buzzing between them. If he could forgive her…

'Why would you want to tell him the truth? To ruin me? Could you imagine how much their wedding would have been worth? The deposit money lost alone could cripple me for the next ten years and you blew it all because you thought *she* wasn't nice enough for him?'

Roxanne bit her bottom lip. Putting it that way was a bit rough. 'But I can't have this hanging over him. He was innocent.'

'Oh, gawd. Get real.' Nadine picked up the soft toys off the chair, bundling them into her arms. 'He *was* unfaithful to his fiancée, just now on the doorstep. He's manipulating you. All he wants is the truth so he can nail you for being a biased, unprofessional liar—ripe for the suing because you ruined his life.'

Nadine's words sliced into her. Either that or he pitied her so much he figured she needed a kiss to boost her confidence or he wanted to be with her, not Heather any more, and wanted to show her that. 'Well, that's debatable…'

'How?'

'He sort of has the impression that I have a broken heart,' she said softly, trying to believe in him. 'And he sort of has a knight complex so he's sort of trying to patch it.'

'Well, he's doing a bang-up job.' Nadine dropped

all the toys into a basket at the end of the sofa, shaking her head. 'The method he's using is quite classic, romancing your vulnerable little self into his arms... probably with only one thing in mind... He's obviously a typical man.'

'Not typical at all. Far from it.' Roxanne tried to smile, touching her lips and feeling the magic fill her chest, warming her. He wasn't like any guy she'd known before.

Nadine stood stock-still, staring at her. 'You don't love him, do you?'

'Of course not.' Roxanne laughed. 'No way.' She shook herself. 'You know I don't fall in love.'

Not a chance. After those failed relationships, since her father cruelly left their mother, broken and alone and since her sister was left stranded with a child, she had vowed she'd never get attached to another man. What made it worse was that her mother hadn't seen it coming. She hadn't suspected anything was wrong with their relationship, their marriage, until the day he had come home from work, packed his bag and left.

It wasn't fair.

She was never going to be like her mother. Who would want to be vulnerable to that sort of pain? No way.

She hated men, all of them, except maybe Cade. He could be different... But then, what if Nadine was right? What if he knew the truth about who she was and what she'd done… Why else would he be so fixed on finding her again?

Just for her? *Unlikely*.

'You do! I can see it written on your face,' Nadine said, slumping on to a corner of the coffee table, facing her, her face softer.

She bit her bottom lip. She couldn't be in love, not with Cade Taylor Watson.

Nadine reached over and held her hands. 'You're a romantic fool, you know. Saving your prince from the evil witch with the idea he'd fall in love with you… Come on, wake up, sis, you know where it's going to lead you—it always does.'

Was that what she'd done? Was she convincing herself he felt something for her because he was everything she wanted in a man…someone who she could imagine taking a risk on?

Nadine stood up. 'What's a man doing with his lips all over yours if he's going to marry another woman? Wants to be with another woman?'

'I don't know.' Her thoughts tumbled. Had she manipulated the situation to suit herself…was she *that* desperate? Was she the evil witch trying to break up the prince and his one true love?

Her eyes stung. The way her luck was, probably.

Nadine squeezed her hands. 'He's either using you or you're using him…' Nadine shook her head. 'End this madness. Okay? You're just going to get hurt. Like Bob hurt me, like our father hurt Mum. Get out while you still can and if you can keep my business safely out of it…I'd be really grateful.'

She nodded slowly, the stab of guilt piercing her chest. Nadine was right. There was no future in it…and risking her sister's livelihood on the long shot of something real was crazy.

One thing they both knew—you couldn't trust a man as far as you could throw him.

Nadine moved beside her on the sofa, wrapping an arm around her. 'If he's spending time with you to get to the truth,' Nadine said softly, sighing, 'he must love her very much.'

'Who?' Roxanne whispered.

'His fiancée. To go through all this to prove his innocence…all this trouble…when the typical guy would just work at romancing himself into her good books with intimate dinners, fancy places, expensive gifts and a healthy dose of sweet nothings.'

Roxanne sagged, her body heavy, her legs weak. Her sister was right. There was only the flaw of the kiss that countered that…unless he was prepared to do *anything* to get the result he wanted.

The kiss was probably her fault, and Rory's and every stupid fairy tale with a prince on a white charger.

Nadine hugged her. 'Cripes, you're notoriously un-lucky in love, aren't you?'

And there was no way she could forget it. The

pain threatened to engulf her. There was only one thing to do.

Put herself out of her misery and end the dream.

Happy ever afters weren't for her, her mother or Nadine.

They lived in the real world.

CHAPTER TWELVE

THE apartment was filled with the sweet aroma of the meal. Cade turned the stereo on and off three times, unsure of whether to go with the mood music or whether it would give Roxanne the wrong idea.

He didn't want that.

He didn't want anything to go wrong.

That kiss had been magical, the surrender in her lips spinning his senses and what was left of his logic out of control.

She was incredible. And he wanted to be with her. He didn't care how or why...she was the one. It pumped through him, fuelling his desire, filling his mind with dreams of a future he couldn't have thought possible.

He couldn't believe in fate. Hadn't believed in it before Roxanne, her dramatic entrance into his life, her amazing eyes, her soft lips...and, hell, however long she needed to get over the bastard who had broken her heart, he was willing to give her.

He could wait.

Cade smoothed out the blue polo shirt he wore over his black trousers, casual yet smart. He cast a look towards the kitchen. Everything was ready.

He was still trying to get around the revelation he'd had. The total error he'd made in assuming he and Heather had enough to make a marriage. She was wonderful and all but now he knew a whole different dimension…and the desire to explore it, and Roxanne, was insatiable.

The rap at the door jolted him.

She was here.

He raked his fingers through his hair, striding to the door, his pulse fast. He couldn't muck this up, not when he'd just discovered what he'd been denying himself in a partner.

She was a friend, a mystery, a rush to his senses that he couldn't have explained or even understood a fortnight ago.

What he'd had with Heather was a shadow compared to this…this was what his parents must have had…this was what the romances on the big screen were filled with. It was what the world thrived on.

This was the rock-the-universe-fireworks type of feeling he'd heard about. He wanted to scream it off the rooftops.

He'd been blind, but now he could see it all clearly—and he was determined not to miss out one moment longer on the magic. He swept open the door.

She was in a simple black singlet top made out of some shiny material with a short black skirt that accentuated every curve of her perfect body, hugging her hips and her waist, taunting him.

Her chestnut hair glistened in the light with high-lights of blond and red, pulled back to her nape by a beaded black clasp.

'Roxanne,' he said softly, holding in the urge to sweep her into his arms and wipe the crease from her forehead with his lips.

He took a deep breath. Control. Patience. They had all the time in the world...there was no need to rush anything. He'd wait for a sign. Any sign that she liked him as much as he was falling for her.

No matter what, he had to take this slow and do it right... She'd been hurt and he didn't want to push her. He'd wait, treasuring every moment she spent with him.

'Cade,' Roxanne whispered, holding her hands tight against her body.

She looked up into his golden eyes, her throat dry. She hadn't thought it would be so hard, seeing him again, knowing the time had come to say goodbye.

She shouldn't have come. She should have wimped out with a phone call or a letter rather than face him again.

Seeing him tortured her soul... He looked incredible...

She flexed her fingers, touching her palm where she'd felt his heart pounding, the heart that belonged to another. The heart she'd misguided and tried to steer into clear waters, the heart she'd deluded herself could be hers.

Nadine was right. She had to keep her feet firmly set on solid ground. Cade was not for her, ever.

She took a deep breath, filling her lungs with the aroma of garlic, onions and tomato. 'Italian?'

'Pizza.' He stepped back and invited her in with a sweep of his hand.

Roxanne moved into the entry of the open-plan apartment, holding her bag in front of her. 'You made pizza?' she asked.

'I made the phone call.' He shrugged, shooting her a boyish grin and slipping his hands deep into his trouser pockets. 'I'm afraid I'm domestically challenged, but I hear that I'm not alone…even Prince Charming orders in.'

'Does he?' She dropped her bag on a table, fighting a smile. How could he make her feel so easy and safe so quickly?

She stepped into the living area, surveying the room. His apartment was like him, larger than life.

Bold blacks, browns and whites struck her. The floor was marbled with rippled white rugs placed strategically around the room delineating the different areas in the loft-style apartment.

Several strong red cushions were set on two brown velour three-seater sofas that sat at right angles to each other, facing an enormously large coffee table with a glass insert and squat brown legs.

The white Venetian blinds at the window were closed, leaving the six-foot-high lamps in the corners of the room to cast the light upwards from their funnels like gigantic tulips.

'You don't look domestically challenged,' she offered. The average guy would not have a house so beautifully decorated, or tidy.

He shrugged. 'I have a lady come in to do the housework.'

'And the decorating?' she asked, her thoughts turning to Heather, who'd probably had the place done for him, gushing about what she figured would suit him and, she had to admit, she'd done it incredibly well.

'Me.' He shrugged. 'It's an architect thing, you know. Aesthetically enthusiastic and all that. Do you like?'

She cast him a long slow look, nodding slowly, trying to fight the satisfaction creeping onto her face that it hadn't been Heather who had read him so well.

As an architect he probably knew something about balance and colour and taste...not just all that technical expertise to keep a building up in strong winds. 'I'm impressed.'

He grinned and nodded towards the kitchen to one side of the room, under an overhanging walkway that looked as if it provided access to several rooms upstairs. 'Are you hungry? Would you like to eat now?'

A pizza box sat on a shiny white counter that stretched like a bar along the length of the kitchen, the sink and the cook top on the other side.

She bit her lip, the thought of sitting through a meal

with the most beautiful man and knowing it was all a lie could just be too much for her.

She couldn't do it. She'd stopped lying to herself a long time ago. About the time when she'd called Aaron on his mobile as she headed south from the church, knowing she could never go up the aisle, never trust a man enough to take the plunge.

She had to be glad Nadine had reminded her before she put herself, and poor Cade, through another disaster.

He deserved so much more.

Roxanne couldn't help but watch him saunter over to the tall metallic stools, pulling one out for her, the round timber seat top awfully inviting.

She could so easily say nothing, to be with him a little longer, to delude herself with her fantasies one last time.

The lie pressed down on her, making it hard to breathe. There was nothing for her here, except more trouble. And only one reason why she'd come.

She faced him, her hands tightly wound in front of her. 'Cade, I can't keep this bottled up any more.'

A shadow flickered across his face, stilling his features. Slowly, his eyes brightened. 'I know what you mean.'

She sighed, relief washing over her. The last thing she could have handled right now was beating about the bush. 'Can we be honest then about our feelings?'

'I'd love us to,' he said, his voice smooth and velvet-soft as he reduced the distance between them.

Roxanne swallowed hard, ignoring her body's jump in temperature. 'We can say what's really on our minds and stop pussyfooting around the truth?'

He moved closer still. 'Absolutely. Let's just pretend that whatever happened before, didn't. It doesn't affect the here and now.'

That seemed like a good idea. Wipe the slate clean…that the kiss had been a mistake…that it had been guilt, pity or maybe even lust—he was a man, after all. 'We should go with what's right.'

'Yes. I feel that too and I feel this is right.'

She nodded. Yes, talking was right, as was giving him the opportunity to get it all off his chest and explain his need for her to tell Heather the truth about that night.

She lifted her chin. 'Yes. And Heather—' She could cope with him confessing his need to get her to meet Heather, cope with him telling her he loved his fiancée utterly and entirely. She could respect that sort of love. Yearned for it.

Maybe she could talk to the woman and explain how much he loved her and make things right for them both.

It felt right, because her own fancies of Cade and her together were just an illusion, a dream that couldn't be.

Cade stood in front of her, looking down at her, his eyes warm and soft. 'It's over.'

She closed her eyes. 'I figured.' Why Heather? She didn't seem to deserve him…but if she was what he wanted, then who was she to argue? Her track record was abysmal, her knowledge of love and relationships a disaster.

He had to know, though, that if Heather wasn't going to see how wonderful he truly was there were choices other than someone who was more than willing to believe the worst of him.

Would he find another woman just like Heather?

She lifted her chin and met his warm gaze. 'Cade, I have to tell you…that you're the most wonderful man that I've ever met.'

His golden eyes glinted with a warmth that made her toes curl. He opened his mouth. She silenced him with her finger on his warm lips.

She had to say this before she went, before she broke the magic, the dream that she held deep in her heart.

'From the first moment I saw you I was struck by your kindness, your warmth, your humour and your amazing smile.'

'Roxanne,' he murmured softly, taking her hand and turning it over in his, planting a kiss in the centre of her palm with his lips.

'Cade…' Her throat tightened, the nerves tingling

all the way up her arm from his goodbye kiss. 'You're not making this easy. I'm trying to tell you that—'

He pulled her close, wrapping his arms around her. 'I know.'

A goodbye hug? She could do that. It didn't mean anything more than his kindness that first day—he was a nice guy.

She slipped her arms around his lean hard body, breathing in his rich cologne and heady male scent. She closed her eyes, holding him, hearing his heart pounding fast and furious where her head rested.

Pounding? She looked up, confusion spinning through her. Why was it pounding? Because he didn't want to pressure her to see Heather? Because he'd miss her?

'Cade—'

He bent down, taking her lips with his, wiping all thought from her mind, sending spirals of sensation coursing down into the pit of her belly, stirring a fire that burnt like molten lava.

Oh, gawd.

Maybe she could have this…just this…he was offering…and he wasn't engaged right now…just to show him that he had choices, offers, a future that didn't have to include a woman like Heather.

A shiver raced down her spine.

She shrugged the sensation off, surrendering to Cade's kiss. It didn't matter that she would give him this, share in this…she knew what he really wanted in the depth of his heart…

It couldn't hurt to let go just for a little while, indulge in the fact that she was his rebound girl, and know that was all she could ever be.

Because tomorrow was goodbye.

CHAPTER THIRTEEN

CADE ran the back of his finger down a lock of Roxanne's silky hair, his breath ragged and his blood raging through his veins.

Now? Now…she wanted him now?

What about slow?

He couldn't believe it. Not only had he run into the woman of his dreams while he'd been blind, he'd found her again and again and now here she was, in his apartment, wanting him, telling him how much she wanted him too.

She looked up at him, her eyes bright, burning with a passion that ripped through him, threatening his control.

Hell, she was special and he thanked the powers that be for the gift of her in his life.

Her rich full lips beckoned. The buttery softness of them still echoed through him, fuelling the fire in the pit of his belly, clawing at his control.

He pulled back. He should probably wait…they had plenty of time. They didn't have to rush into this. They could have walks in the park, on the beach, talking about everything. He wanted to know so much about her, wanted to know everything…

He wanted to savour every second of her, every word she spoke, every smile she made, every touch she gave...

'Cade?' she murmured, her voice soft and lilting as she touched his chest, her palm branding him through his thin shirt.

His body responded to the invitation, his mind warring with the overwhelming urge to throw all care to the wind.

'I don't want to rush—' He cast a look behind him to the bench where the pizza sat, cooling, beside garlic bread and a side salad that he'd agonised over ordering for her. He could have gone fancy French or Thai or Indian, but this felt...right. 'We could eat and talk...talk a lot,' he offered.

She shook her head, a shadow flickering across her face. 'I don't want anything to eat. I don't want to talk.' Her voice broke. 'I only want...you.'

The need swallowed him. He pulled her beautiful body to him, wrapping her in his arms and crushing her mouth under his, drowning in the softness of her, the warmth, the desire that leapt between them.

She was made in heaven.

He lightened the kiss, reining in the hunger. Her mouth softening, her hands sliding around his neck, she pulled him down to her, inviting him back deeper, faster, fiercer.

He was drowning.

She slipped her hands under his shirt, running them

up his bare flesh, sending bolts of desire ripping through him.

He sucked in his breath, pulling back to see her. Did she feel it too?

She smiled, her cheeks flushed, her eyes glinting as she worked his shirt up and off.

He couldn't help but smile with her. For what they both knew they were going to experience. Something incredible. Something special. Something like nothing before.

He leant down, taking the kiss she was offering to him, holding back the desire to take it all.

This was for her. At her pace, not his.

Cade tasted her lips, caressed them with his, teased them, explored them, surrendered to the sizzling currents racing through his body.

She kissed him back, catching his bottom lip, drawing him deeper, closer, wilder.

He couldn't get enough of her lips, or her... He ran his hands down her back, holding her close, fighting the urge to swing her into his arms and carry her to his bed.

Slow... She was a woman to be savoured, a woman he wanted to explore, a woman he wanted to keep.

He skimmed his hands around her, holding her waist, marvelling at her hourglass shape. Wide hips with curves that begged to be touched, a narrow waist that beckoned to be kissed, full breasts that deserved to be worshipped.

Her body was smooth, the fabric of her little black outfit hugging her.

He held her tighter, waves of desire crashing through him. Cripes, it was a thrill to have this effect on her.

'You're so beautiful,' he murmured, trailing kisses from her mouth, along her cheek to the soft part of her neck behind her ear, tasting her soft skin, her sweet scent of vanilla filling his senses. 'But I think we're—'

She ran her hands down his back, down his hot skin to the line of his trousers. 'You think too much.'

Cade pulled back slowly. She may be right. This wasn't a time for thinking. He held her shoulders, traced her curves with his palms, hooking the straps of her chemise top with his fingers and sliding it off and down, revealing the sweet expanse of smooth skin on her stomach, her ribs, her bra, just holding her.

He swallowed hard, his attention caught by the perfection of her breasts, of the soft peach lace just covering her.

Hell.

She smiled, looking up at him with sparkling green eyes that gleamed with something that made his heart contract.

'Roxanne,' he murmured, his voice deep and husky.

He swept her up into his arms and strode through the living area to a door on the far side, nudging the door open with his elbow.

Cade lay her gently on his bed, stepping back, his mind struggling for control.

She reached for him. 'I want you.'

Cade groaned, giving in to the call deep in his body. He peeled off the rest of his clothes and met her open arms, flesh to flesh.

She wanted him.

And he wanted her more than words could say...

Roxanne rested her head on his chest, holding Cade close, listening to his steady breathing, not wanting to let go. She couldn't.

Her entire body buzzed from head to toe from his touch, his lips, his loving.

She wanted more, much more of him...loved him.

She loved him?

She bit her lip, her eyes burning behind her lids. She couldn't...

Cade's arm cradled her against him, his warm breath touching her forehead like a summer's breeze.

She knew it was true.

Roxanne let out a long slow breath, her eyes stinging. She knew this shouldn't have happened, but she loved everything about him. She loved his laugh, his smile, the way he talked about his sister and his parents, the way he cared for her...

She should have told him the truth.

Now it was too late.

But it was better to have lived this lie, loved him and let him go, than never have loved at all.

CHAPTER FOURTEEN

ROXANNE rolled over, snuggling up close against the warm wall of flesh, keeping her eyes closed against the harsh reality that morning brought.

Last night, for most of the night, they had shared each other, talking a little, exploring a lot, a subtle knowing hanging in the air that it was only, and could only be, a dream.

She stretched out, languishing in the tingle of her body, from head to toe. *What a dream.*

If only she could keep sleeping, stay with him, just like this, knowing that in some small way she had touched his life, for better or worse, but hopefully for the better, especially since she wasn't staying.

She knew she couldn't. Or could she?

Had she changed? Could she trust herself this time…could she pursue a future with Cade and know it wasn't a mistake?

There was one thing she wasn't going to do, and that was make a mistake like her mother had. She wasn't going to commit to someone only to have them mercilessly break her heart later when he'd finished with her.

Or worse, be like her father and hurt someone else because you didn't know what you felt.

Never.

She opened her eyes, the first rays of the break of day touching the window, her mind daring to think what she could not say aloud. She loved Cade Taylor Watson.

Already it seemed like a lie. She'd messed up his perfect life by her assumption that Heather wasn't the woman for him. That wasn't love.

She should have been absolutely truthful to Heather and excused herself from the job, let them work it out for themselves.

If she truly loved Cade she'd help him with Heather, but where did that leave her? She didn't know. All she knew was that she had to clear this mess up before she could think about her and Cade...

She had to give him and Heather a fighting chance, for them both to know it was over...to know what they really felt about each other, and she'd let him know that she was there for him, she'd be there waiting when he'd sorted it all out.

She fought the sting behind her eyes. How could she have had the presumption to judge their relationship? She couldn't even choose someone for herself and stick with him long enough to find out if she was right...

She probably *had* been wrong in choosing Aaron, David and Steve as possibilities and right in leaving them, because what she felt now...was incomparable.

Roxanne watched Cade sleep, the expanse of his

coppery skin rising and falling with every breath. He looked as if he loved the beach even more than he'd suggested...

Did Heather know?

She cast a glance towards the door. She should leave, before he woke up, before any embarrassing moments and awkward goodbyes.

She wasn't for him; even if last night was anything more than a healing Band-Aid to a cracked heart and he actually felt something for her, there would be no way he could accept what she'd done. She was having a hard enough time accepting it herself now.

No matter how she thought it, the truth sucked. She had no right to decide who was right for him and who wasn't.

She held the covers tightly against her. What an idiot she had been for not just refusing the job, for not waiting for Heather's relationship with him to run its course...then she would have been free to meet this wonderful man, fall in love with him and be with him.

A buzz of excitement slid through her at the thought. It would have been wonderful, but it could never be.

Roxanne stared at the ceiling. There was no point in thinking about the past. It had been Cade's choice to make and she'd taken that away from him, from both of them, dooming herself to a lonely existence knowing he was out there somewhere...

If he wanted a woman like Heather to be his wife

then who was she to interfere? She wanted him to be happy, wanted him to have what he wanted, and live happily ever after.

Did he love Heather Moreton? Could he still love her after last night? Had he felt the same as she had about the chemistry, the connection that had sparked between them? Or had she just confused his life yet again?

Roxanne scrunched the sheet tightly in her fists. He'd been so insistent that night at the restaurant when he'd first found her that she could feel his goal smouldering under the surface of everything he said and did...until yesterday.

Had things changed? Or had she deluded herself and him into thinking they had?

Was he meant to be with Heather?

Red-hot needles stabbed her at the thought of him with Heather, of him walking down the aisle with her, of them having the perfect little life in the suburbs, growing old together.

She wished it had been her, that she'd met him before Heather, before this mess.

Unless—she held her breath, counting her heart-beats, fighting the sting in her eyes—he didn't love Heather.

'Cade,' she whispered, leaning close, a faint wisp of hope curling around her heart. 'Do you still love Heather?'

He stirred, rolling on to his back, his eyes closed, his breathing deep and slow.

She leant closer. 'Do you still want me to talk to Heather for you?'

His eyelids flickered. 'Hmm? Yes.' He stretched out, yawning. 'Hell, yes, Heather doesn't deserve hurt caused—'

Roxanne's breath snagged in her throat.

That was it then. She folded back the covers. It was so obvious. He was still in love with the woman and had just surrendered to the fact he couldn't have her any more...and there *she* had been.

She slipped out of bed, picking up her clothes as she moved towards the door, her legs getting heavier with each retrieval.

Her sister was right.

She was notoriously bad with men, hopeless at knowing when to hold her cards and when to fold, and she'd done it again.

She'd kept a hand that wasn't even hers, invested her love in the hand despite all warnings, and lost it. She was an idiot to think she would have got anything but pain.

She slipped out the door, her shoes in hand.

The irony clawed at her, that the one man she knew she could commit to, heart and soul, was the one man to whom she never would.

She closed the door quietly behind her. Whatever

she felt didn't mean he had to lose what mattered to him.

By the time she was finished, Heather would be begging him to take her back.

Cade rolled over, the cold bed beside him jolting him from his sleep. He opened his eyes, scanning the room, listening.

She was gone.

He covered his face with his hands, raking his fingers through his hair. He should have expected that. She needed some space...some time to think and feel things through.

Last night had been incredible. A dream...that he could connect so utterly and totally with a woman, so many times.

He swung out of his large empty bed and sat on the edge, holding the covers on either side, breathing deep and slow, just feeling. For the first time ever he felt...complete.

He jerked to his feet and strode to the bathroom and stepped under the shower, his body still charged from last night. He looked back to the bed. He could have loved her a whole lot more today...

Roxanne was his dream come true. Last night had proven it. She wasn't just a friend or an intriguing woman; she was incredible and nothing mattered more to him than being with her.

He leant against the tiles and let the hot water spray

his back and his neck, images of last night filling his mind.

It had been perfect, except for small moments when he'd seen a shadow pass over her face, a sadness, as though she was still thinking of the past.

He'd start doing this thing right. Roxanne deserved to be romanced. She deserved everything. The works. Flowers, chocolates, theatre, galleries and romantic walks on the beach.

His chest tightened. And he'd be just the one to give it to her, show her that she could have her own Prince Charming, that she deserved to be loved and cherished…by him.

He wrenched the taps off, stepping out of the shower, his mind scrambling. *He loved her.* It felt so good to think it, to feel it, and he couldn't wait to tell her.

Hell, he wanted to be with her.

There was only one thing he had to do before he could throw himself completely into this relationship with the most incredible woman on the planet.

There was an obligation that burned inside him. One that he had to make right. Heather. And the sooner he talked to her, the better.

CHAPTER FIFTEEN

ROXANNE stood in front of the office block on the sliver of grass between the footpath and road, her heart thumping madly.

The building was tall, cold and classy, like the woman that she was dreading meeting again, but knew she had to.

She had to do the right thing by Cade.

Just because she couldn't have him didn't mean Heather couldn't. And who knew, she might be a nicer person than Roxanne had first imagined; she might be hiding a beating heart beneath her pristine shell and not have ice for blood.

She had to have something going for her; Cade had proposed to her with the full intention of making her his wife.

She took the lift to the fifth floor, biting down on the end of her thumbnail. So, the woman had been awfully keen to accept Cade's betrayal of her; she might just have been insecure, and had hidden that insecurity complex really well under the bitch façade. It didn't mean this quest was hopeless.

She had to give Heather and Cade a chance to work it out, with all the facts out in the open, and only then…maybe…there'd be a chance for them.

The office suite was exquisite. Plush cream lounge suites sat opposite the bank of lifts, giving the impression of a department store display as soon as you stepped out. Brand new magazines were piled neatly on the coffee tables and there was enough foliage in the room to make you think you were in a park.

It was as far removed from Nadine's shoebox as you could get. The woman could have afforded to go somewhere a little classier than to her sister's for help, unless she didn't want the best in the business.

'I'd like to see Miss Moreton, please,' she offered the woman who walked up the hall towards the receptionist's desk.

She glanced around her at the incredibly large plants littering the room, half smothering the seating area in greenery. If they got any bigger they'd have to bring in a gardener.

'Have you got an appointment?' the woman asked, sitting down.

Roxanne clasped her hands in front of her. 'No.'

The woman at the desk lifted an eyebrow, the message screaming loud and clear. 'I'm sorry madam, but—'

'Give her this... She'll see me.' She passed Nadine's business card over to the woman. She should have rung so she didn't have to rely on her sister's business card to get her in the door.

She had wanted to keep Nadine out of this.

The receptionist looked at the card, then at Roxanne. 'You're a private investigator?'

'Affiliated.'

'One moment, please.' The receptionist punched a number on the phone, turning away slightly to talk.

The room filled with tension...she must have been oozing it, her neck prickled.

Would Heather see her? Would curiosity be enough to get her out here to talk to her?

'I thought our business was over,' a familiar voice said behind her.

Roxanne turned to Heather Moreton, who was looking just as icy as she remembered. Her hair was pulled severely back and knotted at her nape to within an inch of its life, her three-piece grey suit impeccably tailored for the woman's long, lithe body.

Roxanne swallowed hard. How could she even compare with her? 'Miss Moreton,' she began. Should she go with pleasantries, the weather, or straight to the point? 'Wouldn't you like to discuss this in private?'

Heather flicked a piece of lint off the shoulder of her suit. 'I may need a witness. Did I or did I not pay you for the services you rendered?'

'Yes, but—' She sucked in a deep breath. This was it. Crunch time. She looked skyward and prayed for forgiveness from Nadine, Rory's face jumping to her mind's eye.

She shook herself. She'd do anything...sell her car, work twenty-four-seven, give her everything she had…to put things right again for Cade. 'But the report wasn't entirely accurate.'

Heather crossed her arms over her chest. 'Are you saying Cade didn't hit on you?'

'That's right,' she said in a rush, nodding furiously. 'I'm sorry, but you were so insistent…and I misunderstood your impatience for a result for wanting only a *certain* result.'

'It doesn't matter.' Heather waved her off like an annoying insect and glanced at her watch. 'Is there anything else?'

'What do you mean?' Roxanne stepped back, blinking, looking over the woman again as though she was seeing her for the first time. 'I'm saying that in an effort to please you I over-exaggerated…the truth is Cade was a gentleman…' She took a deep breath, steeling herself. 'You can get back with Cade.'

'Get back with him?' Heather laughed. 'Are you nuts? No. I found the most incredible guy on my trip to Madrid two months ago and have been trying to get out of marrying Cade ever since.'

Roxanne's chest tightened and her eyes stung. Poor loving Cade. 'You used me as an excuse to break up with him?' she asked dully.

'Absolutely. I couldn't have all my friends and colleagues thinking I was a two-timing hussy.' She straightened the white cuffs of her shirt, which were poking out from under her jacket. 'Better they think he ruined our beautiful wedding.' She nodded, a smile tugging at her thin mouth. 'It all worked out brilliantly, actually, thanks to you.'

Roxanne held her stomach, fighting the engulfing numbness. *She'd been a part of this…game?* 'What about Cade?'

Heather clicked her tongue. 'Cade will be fine, silly. If you didn't notice, he's quite okay… He'll find someone else to fit into his neat little life.' Heather raised her finely pencilled eyebrows. 'Now, if you've quite finished clearing your conscience, I have work to do.'

'But Cade—' she began. It couldn't just end like this, not when Cade had loved this woman so dearly and so utterly…

The woman paused, her eyes narrowing.

Roxanne caught herself. She could see the cogs falling into place for the shrewd woman. She wasn't stupid…she had to see there wasn't much chance that conscience and work ethic had had her traipsing halfway across town to see her a month after their original meeting.

She touched her forehead, wondering if her love for Cade was written plainly there. It had better not be. 'You're right,' she blurted, crossing her fingers mentally that it wasn't too late to save the situation. 'A tall arrogant piece of meat like that will find a willing woman anywhere.'

Heather nodded, her gaze wary. 'He's a real charmer when he wants to be.'

Roxanne stepped back, smoothing out her black trousers, wishing she'd never come. There was no way she had to risk Nadine's future over this, not now, not when Heather didn't even care.

She licked her lips, her mind scrambling for the right words to allay the woman's suspicions. 'Wouldn't mind a piece of him myself…but he's out of my league…I'm not anywhere near *your* class.'

Heather fluttered her eyelashes and touched her *coiffure*. 'True.'

She mentally crossed her fingers that the flattery was enough. 'Thanks for your time…just wanted to rid that albatross from around my neck.'

The woman nodded.

Roxanne turned and fled, a thousand screams needing to be voiced. Cade wasn't going to have his happy-ever-after with Heather that he was working so hard for.

She punched the lift button. The sweet thought of being free to love him drifted through her mind.

Was it possible? If she confessed what she'd done, if she bared her heart and soul to him, if she trusted him not to break hers?

Could he love her? She dared to consider the possibility, that the reason he had spent time with her wasn't for Heather, it was for him, that the reason he had made mad passionate love to her all night wasn't because he wanted to, but because he *needed* her.

She'd been brave enough to face the ice queen.

Why not face the man she loved, trust him with the truth, her sister's business and her heart, and pray that he was her prince and they'd live happily ever after?

She couldn't help but smile. She could be Cinderella who'd finally found happiness.

Maybe fairy tales could come true.

Cade stood up, folding back the errant frond of rubber plant that had all but smothered him while he had been waiting, his body filled with a cold dread that lapped his heart.

Why in hell had he waited? He should have just walked straight into Heather's office and come clean, told her that although he'd been innocent before, he wasn't now, and explained to her that it was best for both of them this way.

He had been a fool. He could see Heather's little-miss-sweet-and-friendly act for what it was, clearly—an act. To get what she had wanted…him. Until someone better had come along.

Hearing Roxanne's voice in a place she couldn't possibly be had sliced right through him. He hadn't been able to do anything, frozen to the seat, the conversation crashing like meteors into his chest.

He clenched his fists by his sides with anger. The woman he *had* thought he loved had paid the woman he loved to set him up.

Nothing was clearer. He was an idiot. Used.

Dumped. Used. And undoubtedly, when Roxanne was finished with him, dumped.

She'd been an award-winning actress, had him convinced of her vulnerability. Her need for some kindness and her need for someone to love her.

Dammit.

Thank God he hadn't told her what he felt for her. Who knew what she would have pulled next on him. For what? Her own entertainment?

He sucked in a quick breath, looking over to Heather, who was talking to the receptionist, shuffling papers.

Heather knew he'd been blameless and it hadn't mattered to her. Hadn't changed a thing. The whole ordeal for the benefit of her image…the guilt he'd wrestled with over the last few weeks nothing to her.

What he had suffered over his growing attraction to another woman, his supposed betrayal of her…

His blood boiled.

Cade pushed the frond out of the way, stalking to where the woman he'd been going to marry stood with her receptionist sorting messages.

'Heather.'

She swung around, eyes wide. 'Cade,' she said tightly, darting a glance to the lifts. 'What are you doing here?'

'Cut the crap. I heard it all,' he said between gritted teeth, hands by his sides, clenched tight. 'I have one question.'

She nodded soberly, her body stiff as though she was bracing herself for a tornado, or worse, litigation.

'Who was she?'

Heather sighed. 'She's a professional...you know, the sort of person you hire to sit around in a bar and seduce your guy when he shouldn't even be looking.'

The words were like punches. He'd missed the start of the conversation. He'd been obsessed with his own spiel, not who was talking quietly back there.

He'd been so played. Was such an idiot. He'd fallen for Roxanne's whole routine and had been stupid enough to feel sorry for her.

No wonder she had been so surprised to see him turn up in her life. Again and again. What he had thought was fear of commitment was actually fear of discovery.

He stared at the woman he'd thought he would marry. At least, until he'd met Roxanne, who'd shown him the extra dimensions he hadn't even considered.

Dimensions that were as illusory as Escher's impossible perspective pictures, like 'Relativity'.

'Goodbye, Heather,' he said, nodding grimly. He didn't need to know anything else. What else was there to know—what *price* had she asked for the deception?

'Look, Cade. I'm sorry,' she offered.

He shook his head. 'Sorry isn't enough.' Not by a long shot. How could she not have come to him and just explained herself? He would have understood. He wouldn't have blamed her.

He swung around and strode to the exit. How could she hire someone? Like Roxanne…the beautiful, enchanting…lying manipulator.

He took the stairs, striding down three at a time, concentrating on the stained concrete beneath him rather than the harsh words of their conversation echoing in his head.

He hadn't heard everything… Roxanne had probably offered Heather the additional information she had collected to solidify her earlier report—the erroneous one—and she'd dismissed it as unnecessary.

He should have known something had been different since that last trip Heather had taken overseas. She'd cut down their dates, become a little more distant, more pensive.

Why couldn't he have seen these things? It was all so obvious now, even Roxanne and her games.

Fate! Roxanne would have thought him a fool thinking their meeting again was fate. The only thing fated about their meeting was Heather helping Roxanne fashion herself into the sort of woman that would not only interest him but compromise all the values he held dear to be with her.

If Roxanne hadn't been in such a rush there would have been no need for a lie to Heather. It would only have been a matter of time before he fell head over heels for her. There would have been no need for him to chase Roxanne either because he would have known he was guilty as sin.

He flexed his fingers, the memory of her smooth skin sliding under his touch, the buttery taste of her lips, the sweet scent of her skin.

It was probably about the money. And she couldn't wait. And he'd been an idiot and chased her round the place to give her the rest to assuage her conscience.

He gritted his teeth against the ache sucking in his guts, his heart and his soul. He should have stuck with logic and left well enough alone.

He pushed through to the lobby and strode into the dreary overcast day. He turned back towards his office. It was the only answer. Always had been. Work had kept him busy and occupied, distracted from what was missing in his life.

He needed it now more than ever.

Cade stalked down the street, each step pounding the reality into his brain. Roxanne and him weren't ever going to have a future. She was an actress out for the money and he was an albatross around her neck.

He'd been seduced by an illusion.

But it was over.

Her case completed.

Better to find out before he did something any more stupid than he had already, like tell the seductress that he loved her.

At least he'd never have to see her again.

CHAPTER SIXTEEN

ROXANNE paced on the front step of Nadine's house, smoothing out her plain black dress, gnawing on what was left of her fingernails, glancing up and down the road, the street lights twinkling like diamonds.

She put her hands behind her back, her insides jangling. She couldn't wait to see him again...

Anticipation beat through her as clearly as the knowledge that she finally had a chance at love. A real chance. Could she ever have thought it possible? Were there enough signs to know she had a future with him? Did it matter? She had to do this.

She'd found a man she could love so totally and utterly that there was no way that committing to him could be wrong.

All she had to do was trust in him.

Where was the taxi? She glanced back to the lights in the house. She hadn't told Nadine the latest turn of events. She couldn't risk her sister talking her out of taking this gamble, didn't want her to know that she was going to tell Cade everything and have her worry unnecessarily.

She crossed her fingers. *Please let this be okay.*

All the messages screamed it was time for her to

jump, parachute or not. That of all men, this man was the one who she could trust with her heart, the one that would stick by her, *if* he loved her.

That was all she had to find out. If he still loved Heather or could love her—did love her?

Roxanne's neck prickled. She swung around. Had Nadine sensed what was going on?

Rory stood at the door, holding it, staring at her, a funny little smile on her face. 'You're going to the ball.'

Roxanne nodded, trying not to smile.

'Are you going to let him rescue you?' she asked, stepping forward and slipping her hand into hers. 'It's okay to be rescued. Mummy needs rescuing, she just doesn't know it yet.'

'I know,' she said softly, glancing up as the taxi arrived. 'Wish me luck.'

'Here.' Rory thrust a small pink stick towards her, hardly longer than a pencil. 'Take my wand…it's better than luck.'

Roxanne nodded, stowing the stick in her purse, running her hand down her niece's cheek, her heart aching for the insight she had for one so young.

'The star fell off but I think it still works.'

Roxanne couldn't help but smile, walking down to the kerb and waving goodbye like Cinderella did to her fairy godmother, all three feet six inches of her.

Her stomach was full of butterflies but she had a

dream for a life filled with love and happiness tucked in her purse with the wand.

Magic was in the air.

Roxanne stood staring at Cade's apartment door, wondering what to say, how to say it and how to make the truth sound sweeter than it was.

Maybe she should have waited until he'd called her, dropped in or written. What if last night was all there was? What happened if she'd just been a good time?

No. He wasn't like that.

She glanced back at the stairs. It may have been wiser to wait, to let him call her and initiate the next meeting...so she knew he cared about her, so she knew that telling him everything was worth the risk.

She looked at his door. So much depended on how he felt towards her, and Heather...and how could she tell him the truth without affecting his last girlfriend?

Cade had such a high regard for Heather...but then, he was the most understanding man she'd ever met. He was sure to appreciate his fiancée falling for someone else, but maybe not the way she had gone about extricating herself from him.

'Roxanne.'

She jumped at the deep, familiar voice behind her, ricocheting through her like a bullet in a cave filled with bats.

She swung around to face Cade.

He wore a business suit that was as superbly tailored as the first one she'd seen him in. His tie was loose as though he'd yanked at it and his hair was ruffled.

He looked tired. She tipped her head, holding herself still, half tempted to fall into his arms and hold him.

'Cade,' she said in a rush, glancing from her watch to his door, to him. It was late to have still been working… 'Where have you been?'

'Work,' he stated flatly, not meeting her gaze, shuffling his hands around his suit pockets. 'I've been working. Work means a lot to me. I sometimes get consumed by it. Don't know any boundaries and don't care…but then you'd know that feeling.'

Roxanne saw a shadow in his golden eyes, saw that the smile had gone from his face and was vividly aware of the lack of enthusiasm in his tone. Had leaving him this morning been the wrong thing to do? Had she hurt him?

'Last night was wonderful,' she blurted, holding in the urge to go to him and kiss his gorgeous lips, wrap her arms around him, rest her head on his chest and hear the steady thrum of his heart.

He stood like a block of stone, his eyes moving over her like a stranger's, coldly taking in her dress.

The look jarred. 'Cade?' She stepped forward. What was wrong? More than a hurried exit this morning…despite it being a workday, and he had to see how awkward this morning had been for her, them. With Heather and all…

He jerked forward, moving past her towards his door, making no gesture to register the intimacy that they'd shared.

'Cade?'

He pulled out a set of keys and flicked through them. 'What do you want?'

Roxanne's eyes burned. 'I wanted to see you. Talk to you.' The bitter truth slithered through her veins, chilling her body. 'There's so much to say.'

He glanced at her. 'Not as far as I'm concerned.' He turned his attention back to his keys. 'Look, last night was pretty nice. A good rumble under the covers, but that's about it.'

Roxanne stared at his wide back, her vision blurring. Had she been so wrong? 'You still love Heather?' she asked, the words clogging in her throat.

'Yeah, sure.' He stabbed the key into his lock and pushed open the door. 'But don't feel bad. You were a great distraction from her dumping me and it was great to let off steam.'

She opened her mouth, closed it, feeling empty inside. What else had she expected? He was a man.

Her eyes burned. He wasn't different at all; he was the same, the same as all the men who had hurt her in her life, like her father had hurt them all.

No. She lifted her chin. Whatever the reason, it didn't matter. She still loved him… 'I'm glad I could help some.' She turned away, biting her bottom lip to stop the cry from escaping her throat.

Her legs were like jelly.

This couldn't be real, not when she'd been so happy, so incredibly thrilled at finding him...not when she loved him so much, and not when she had Rory's magic wand in her purse.

She swung around. Her sister had found faith to marry her husband and have Rory, her mother had found the strength to trust her father and made them both, despite the odds.

It was her turn to be brave and it was now or never. Sure, both her mother and sister had lost love, but it didn't mean her future was written, that she was doomed too.

'Cade, I just want to say—' She swallowed hard, lifting her gaze to meet his cold one. 'That the time that we've had together has meant a lot to me.'

He leant against the doorjamb, crossing his arms over his chest. 'Right.'

She closed her eyes against the crash of pain at his easy dismissal. 'And that I love you.'

'Anything else?' He glanced at his watch. 'I have things to do.'

'No,' she said softly, shaking her head. She'd been half-expecting a reaction—stunned silence, fireworks or an on-your-knees declaration of his feelings.

He didn't care enough.

She closed her eyes and thought how lucky Heather was still to have his love.

This was just another disaster.

Or maybe just the wrong time? Maybe later…? 'I'm around… If you ever need a friend—'

He shrugged. 'I've got enough. Thanks.'

His words slammed into her, taking her breath away.

Roxanne stared at him for one moment, swung around and hurried away, the tears breaking through the dam and spilling down her cheeks.

She'd done it.

She'd taken the risk and bared her heart, and lost.

She wasn't like Cinderella at all now. Cinderella knew the prince had her glass slipper, that there was a chance that the dream could come true.

For Roxanne there was nothing, except regrets.

CHAPTER SEVENTEEN

CADE slammed his office door, clutching his coat jacket tightly, striding through the office, his eyes on the floor.

There were no cheery goodnights from any of the staff or his partners. He didn't blame them. He was like a tyrannosaurus with sore teeth. Dangerous.

He knew it. But couldn't help it. Something churned deep inside him, clawing at him, wearing at him, making everything grate on him and making life hell for everyone around him.

He balled his fists. It couldn't be because of Roxanne. That was done and finished. Over, three days, eight hours and forty-eight minutes ago.

He punched the lift button. He'd done the right thing. He'd made sure she knew that she'd done a good job...had been a great actress and seduced him good and proper and she was great in bed. But he was no one's fool.

The love thing had come out of left field. Part of the mind-twisting game she'd been playing, or what? He didn't know.

Hell, he didn't want to know. She'd used him. Her *and* Heather...but she was the worst. Making out she was his friend. That she liked him. Needed him even.

He'd been played like an idiot.

He stepped into the lift and stabbed the button for the basement garage. What had possessed him to go looking for more trouble with the woman? And, dammit, he'd found it. In her eyes, in her arms and in her lips.

He'd thought all his dreams had come true…that he'd finally found someone special to share his life with.

He shook his head. No wonder the woman had confused the hell out of him from the moment he'd met her…see-sawing from confident seductress to guarded ally…she probably hadn't known what to make of his enthusiasm to give her the opportunity to stick another knife in.

The doors of the lift slid open.

Roxanne's face leapt to his mind, a vision, her hair flowing around her shoulders, glistening with reds and blonds in the light that had been on his landing.

He hadn't missed the sadness in her eyes. The way she bit her bottom lip. The glisten in her eyes.

Real or just part of the act?

Why keep acting? Wasn't it over? Hadn't that meeting with Heather been the signal to end the charade? Was that what she had been going to do at his front door and he'd robbed her of the opportunity to make it a dramatic exit?

Cade stalked to his car. He didn't want to feel like this. He didn't like doubts. Guilt.

That look in her eyes was haunting him.

His gut twisted. She'd appeared wounded by his words... Had he *hurt* her?

Was it possible to hurt a woman like that?

Was there any way to get to a woman like her or had he slipped between the cracks and seen the real woman beneath the ruthless professional?

Was Rory part of the act, what she'd said, or was it the sad and sorry reason a pretty woman like Roxanne would choose such a bitter, cynical, manipulating job?

He clenched his fists by his sides. He had to know.

Somehow he had to find out.

He needed help, someone with experience. And he knew just who to call.

Roxanne stared at the prints on the walls of the gallery, hardly seeing the pictures at all. They weren't buildings—that exhibition was over—as were all her hopes and dreams.

She'd never felt this empty in her life. Her body was heavy, as though it was filled with lead, and her chest was void, as though a black hole had ripped through her and sucked everything that mattered out of her.

Sure, she still had her sister. Obsessive, controlling Nadine who was keeping her hard at work until another job came up for her. The paperwork in her office was endless.

Rory was a doll. She'd taken one look at her that night and shaken her head, patting her on the arm. 'Bad ball, huh?' she'd said.

Roxanne had kept it together enough to make it to her room before the tears had come. And they'd come. All night, every night and every time she thought of him, which was too often.

She hadn't talked much to her niece, had tried to avoid her, her failure driving deeper every time she looked at the little girl. What effect did it have on Rory's ideals, on her own sad and sorry future in love?

She sighed, staring at the photo of a couple on a bench, looking as though they'd sprouted there like mushrooms and grown old there together.

She tried to breathe, her chest tight. All the times she'd thought she had a broken heart were nothing compared to this. The world seemed to have lost colour, purpose and meaning.

No wonder her mother had given up.

No wonder it made sense not to get involved.

Had Nadine felt this way when she'd found out that her husband was cheating on her? Had she struggled with her stupid decision to marry the guy and have his child? Yet her sister survived anyway.

Had her mother felt this emptiness and drowned in it?

Her eyes stung. At least they'd had the love for a while, the dream for a short time, some good times to hang on to to keep them going, to give them hope.

She had nothing but a fleeting moment in time. One night. And she knew she should be glad of it, that no matter how small that loving interaction, that sharing and joining of body and soul, they'd shared the magic. Some people went their entire lives without experiencing it, and she could go the rest of hers without another taste.

Day in day out, she just had to keep breathing. Living.

She'd found herself in Harry's bar yesterday for no reason, being jostled by a bunch of suits she didn't know, being propositioned by guys who weren't Cade.

The night before she'd found herself ordering cannelloni from a certain Italian restaurant and taking it home. She hadn't been able to eat it. She'd just sat and looked at it until Pumpkin couldn't cope with the anticipation any longer and jumped on the chair and ate the thing.

Roxanne moved to the next print, staring blankly, unseeing, looking around her in the quiet gallery, trying to recapture just a tiny portion of what she'd shared with Cade before the dream had crashed down around her.

'Hey.' A young woman sidled up beside her. 'That's not one of the crying ones. You'll upset the artist.'

Roxanne frowned, touched her cheeks and pulled back her hand, her fingers damp. 'I'm sorry.'

'Correct me if I'm wrong but aren't you the woman

who bought one of those linearly inspired building prints?'

She nodded. She'd hung it over her bed, staring up at it for hours with the street lights shining in on the surface, highlighting the angular shapes, reminding her of Cade and how far out of reach he'd been.

'The woman that my brother was trying to find?' the young woman asked, tipping her head.

Roxanne stepped back, turning, looking towards the door and around her. Of course. She'd forgotten…how could she have forgotten that this was his sister's gallery?

The young woman frowned. 'You're the one who broke his heart.'

'Broke *his* heart?' She shook her head. 'No, you're thinking of Heather Moreton. Did he try to get back with her?' She stomped her foot. 'I should've warned him that she had someone else.'

The young woman tilted her head. 'Sounds like you care about him.'

Roxanne backed away, shaking her head. 'Just as a friend…' she said, choking on the words he hadn't wanted to hear either. 'He needed someone to…no one deserves to get hurt like that.'

'No,' his sister said, her eyes narrowing. 'They don't.'

'I have to go.' Roxanne swung around and strode out of the gallery, away from Cade's sister, away from the memories she was fighting with.

She should just try to shove the memory of him with the others who'd travelled through her life. There was no reason to hold him close to her heart as a dream that could've been, but wasn't.

She had to get on with it, like Nadine, get stronger and thick-skinned, because there was bound to be more foul weather in her future.

She had to grow up and get tough. She was living in the real world and knights in shining armour only existed in fairy tales.

No one was going to save the damsel in distress, except the damsel herself.

She had to sort out her own life, her own fears and know that she'd be okay. In time the pain of this would fade. One day...in a time far, far away.

CHAPTER EIGHTEEN

RORY stood at the window, playing dolls on the windowsill, one dressed up in a glittering gold gown with a wedding veil, the boy doll with a purple cape that flowed behind him.

Roxanne jerked her attention back to the letter she was typing on her laptop, trying not to watch the girl. It was torture.

There was nothing wrong with believing in fairy tales if you were nearly five...nearly twenty-five, a whole different matter.

She tried to focus on the screen, resigned to the fact that she couldn't stay at Nadine's for ever. She had to break away from the only family she had left and stand on her own two feet again.

It was nice to belong, though, nicer still to share with someone the woes of the day, but her sister had her life and Roxanne had to go and remake her own.

'You're crying again,' Rory sung, stuffing a handful of tissues at her.

What was wrong with her? She wasn't this person. She was strong and tough and got on with life. She had every other time...

'Don't worry, Aunty Rox.' Rory patted her small

hand on Roxanne's. 'He'll come. Princes always do. One girl had to wait, like a hundred days.'

'Years,' Roxanne corrected, dabbing her eyes, trying to smile at her niece. Would she have to wait that long for another chance at love?

She wiped her face and looked back at her résumé, determined to concentrate on work…it was all she had left.

The doorbell chimed.

Rory leapt off the couch. 'Me, me,' she yelled, running to the door as though it was a race.

Roxanne hadn't moved. She didn't want to see anyone. She stared towards the hall, focusing on the rattle of the lock and the door.

She hoped it was one of Nadine's friends and not someone she had to get off the couch for.

'She's been waiting for you for ever so long,' Rory's small voice sang. 'And crying everywhere. I gave her my wand but I don't think she knows how to use it.'

Roxanne's heart leapt into her throat.

No.

She slammed down the screen, swinging the laptop to one side on to the cushions, jerking to her feet. Her legs were like jelly, unable to hold her weight. She sagged back down on to the seat, her heart pounding like a violent storm raging inside her chest.

It could be Rory still playing make-believe, with Pumpkin, a salesman, or Nadine?

She glanced at the dolls lying on the windowsill.

Rory swung around the corner, jumping up and down on the spot. 'He's come for you. He's come.'

Cade stepped out and stood behind Rory, his shoulders stiff, his hands deep in his trouser pockets. His eyes were shadowed, his hair ruffled and his face drawn. 'I came to talk.'

Rory smiled, backing out of the room. 'I told you princes come, even the slow ones.' She looked up at Cade. 'You're a slow one, but she would have waited a hundred years.'

Roxanne opened her mouth, her cheeks heating. She looked up to the ceiling blinking madly, wishing her legs were stronger and that the door was closer.

Cade stepped forward. 'I couldn't stop thinking about everything. You, Heather, everything... I tried to deny it, tried to fight it, but I couldn't get you out of my head.'

Roxanne held herself still, her mind tumbling over his words. What?

He threw a thumb to his right. 'I stopped in to see Petra, my sister, for her advice. She's been through a fair bit with relationships. The optimist of the family, I think. She told me you'd been by.'

She stared at him, watching him run his hands through his hair, watching the heavy rise and fall of his chest, the slight tinge on the tips of his ears, the tension in him. 'I need to know what the hell your game was, is.'

'Game?' she whispered, hardly daring to breathe. Was this a dream or a nightmare that was only going to hurt her more?

He sighed heavily. 'I know you were paid to seduce me so Heather could cut me loose.'

'Oh, gawd.' She stared at him, fighting the sensation of her stomach dropping out from beneath her. Was he here to serve a legal document on her for wrecking his life? 'How?' she asked tightly.

He strode across the room to the window. 'I was there, Roxanne. The *albatross* was in the waiting room behind those stupid plants.'

She covered her mouth. No. He'd heard *that*? Her throat ached. 'Cade…' she choked. 'I was trying to put Heather off the idea that I'd misled her deliberately so she wouldn't sue my sister.'

'Did you?'

'Yes. I…' She shook her head, trying to think of an excuse for not doing this, for not confessing her stupidity or how much she loved him. 'Cripes. Cade, you didn't want to be with her. She was evil. I told her what she wanted to hear to save you from a fate worse than death.'

His mouth pulled thin and he crossed his arms over his formidable chest.

'I know that was wrong, that it should have been your choice, that you and Heather should have discussed the situation and worked it out, without interference. But she wouldn't listen. No matter how much I suggested it, she insisted on using us.'

Cade watched her, silent.

'I just couldn't help myself,' she rushed on. 'You were a wonderful person and didn't deserve what Heather was doing.'

'But you told her a lie,' he stated tightly.

Roxanne looked at her lap, her hands clasped tightly together. 'I told her what she wanted to hear, with no intention of pursuing you, honestly.'

'You didn't.'

She glanced up at him. 'No. Then you turned up, wounded and searching for the truth…and the more time I spent with you the more I wanted to stay with you.'

'You did?' Cade said, moving closer.

She jerked to her feet, lifting her chin and facing the one man she knew who wouldn't be a mistake…if only…

Roxanne sucked in a long slow breath, smothering her past mistakes, her fears, her family's fate. 'Yes. I fell in love with you, okay? I know I mean absolutely nothing to you, that I lied, that I hurt you by that lie…but I can't help what I feel.'

'You love me?' he echoed. '*Really* love me?'

'I know I'm screwed up, know that my parents were crappy role models, that Nadine's marriage break up didn't help, that all the guys I couldn't commit to probably hate me, like you do. But I have trouble trusting people with my heart, okay? I thought it was just because I was scared of becoming my mother, but it wasn't. I was scared of becoming my father and hurting someone as cruelly as he did.'

Roxanne took a deep breath. 'And I know I messed it up. I hardly knew you and I screwed it up, hurt you by damaging the relationship you had with Heather.' She spread her arms wide. 'So, now you know everything.'

Cade watched her, his eyes giving nothing away.

'Well, say something... What are you doing here?' she demanded, glaring at him. How could he be so cruel as to drag this out...? Did he want to make her suffer because Heather had found someone else? 'Heather?'

'I don't love Heather.'

'You don't?' she breathed. Because Heather didn't love him any more? Because he hated her? Them both? All women?

'No.' Cade grabbed her shoulders. 'But I get it.'

Her breath caught in her throat. He did? She didn't. She was as confused as ever.

He ran the back of his hand down her cheek. 'You know you just told me you love me,' he said slowly. 'You said that before, last Monday night...'

She stared up into his golden eyes, not daring to breathe. 'Ye-es.'

'So, you are trusting *me*?'

Roxanne nodded, taking a deep slow breath. 'I'm

willing to risk my heart, again and again, *for you* because you complete me. You touch my soul and make me yearn that every minute with you is an eternity.'

Cade's eyes glittered, his mouth curving.

Rory slipped up to Cade and pulled his sleeve, handing him one of Roxanne's slippers. 'This will help.'

Cade frowned, taking the offering from Rory, whose grin stretched across her face.

Roxanne dropped into the seat behind her, relief washing through her. He didn't hate her, then… She could get on with life feeling better, knowing he didn't hate her.

Cade dropped to his knees in front of her.

She stared at him, taking a quick breath. What?

He smiled up at her, bending over and catching her right foot. 'I've been a rotten prince. I ignored my heart and wouldn't let you tell me the truth.' He pushed the large pink fluffy slipper on to her foot. 'I'm sorry. Could you ever forgive me?'

Roxanne touched his jaw with her fingertips, staring into those eyes that she thought she'd never see again, her eyes blurring, her throat stinging.

Could this be happening?

'You rocked my world the moment you told me I ran through your dreams.' He ran his hand around her neck, drawing closer to her. 'You shattered my illusions about love, taught me what it is to feel, want, yearn, to be with someone.'

She took a ragged breath, her chest filling with an incredible warmth.

He drew her down to him. 'I love you so incredibly much that I ache to hold you.'

She couldn't help but smile. 'Hold me then,' she whispered to her prince.

Roxanne didn't have to worry about being hurt like her mother or hurting like her father had. She wasn't cursed to live her mother's pain. This was her life and she was going to love for as long and as much as she could.

She had her knight in shining armour, the man who had proven that fairy tales could come true, that dreams were made to be found and loved and trusted.

Cade swept Roxanne into his arms, wrapping his arms around her, pulling her close. His body heated at her touch, her arms around him, the contact that he'd longed for.

'Kiss her,' Rory whispered.

Cade obliged. He bent his head, taking Roxanne's lips and making his claim on the woman who had shown him what love truly was.

She'd saved him from Heather because she liked him. Had saved him from himself because he'd been a fool. And had sacrificed herself because she loved him.

He pulled back. 'Will you forgive me for being a very slow prince who should've listened to his heart rather than his head?'

She nodded, her eyes glistening, her lips full and moist and beckoning. 'If you can forgive me for meddling in your life.'

'Done.' He drew her close, brushing her lips again, savouring her warmth, her softness, her sweet vanilla scent that had haunted him since he'd first met her.

'Friends?' she asked cautiously.

'No.' He brushed a strand of hair back from her face, staring down into her emerald eyes, which were gleaming with the love that he couldn't have possibly fathomed existed. 'As much more than friends...as my one and only princess.'

'I'm a princess too,' Rory piped up.

Cade smiled at the little girl. 'That you are. And you'll find a knight in shining armour one day.'

'Nope.' She shook her head, her pigtails swishing around her face. 'I want a frog. More fun. And when I want a prince I just have to kiss him. I don't have to wait around or look for him.'

Cade couldn't help but laugh. 'Good idea.'

'I wish I'd thought of that.' Roxanne smiled.

'I'm late, but I'm here.' He looked at the woman in his arms. 'Do you want to ride off into the sunset with me?'

She trailed her fingers down his jaw, her smile reflected in the brightness of her eyes that shone just for him. 'How can I refuse?'

MILLS & BOON®

Modern *Extra*
romance™

More passion for your money!

In August, Mills & Boon Modern Romance is
proud to bring back by popular request,
Raising the Stakes,
and have added a new-in-print linked story,
The Runaway Mistress,
as a bonus. Both come from bestselling,
award-winning author
Sandra Marton.

Sandra has written more than 50 Modern
Romances and her Barons stories have
pleased many readers:

'**An unforgettable read overflowing with
exciting characters, a powerful premise and
smouldering scenes.**'
–*Romantic Times*

MILLS & BOON

EMMA DARCY

Kings of Australia

'Nothing will stop this breed of men from winning the women they love'

On sale 5th August 2005

Available at most branches of WHSmith, Tesco, ASDA, Martins, Borders, Eason, Sainsbury's and all good paperback bookshops.

4 FREE

BOOKS AND A SURPRISE GIFT!

We would like to take this opportunity to thank you for reading this Mills & Boon® book by offering you the chance to take FOUR more specially selected titles from the Tender Romance™ series absolutely FREE! We're also making this offer to introduce you to the benefits of the Reader Service™—

- ★ FREE home delivery
- ★ FREE gifts and competitions
- ★ FREE monthly Newsletter
- ★ Exclusive Reader Service offers
- ★ Books available before they're in the shops

Accepting these FREE books and gift places you under no obligation to buy, you may cancel at any time, even after receiving your free shipment. Simply complete your details below and return the entire page to the address below. You don't even need a stamp!

YES! Please send me 4 free Tender Romance books and a surprise gift. I understand that unless you hear from me, I will receive 6 superb new titles every month for just £2.75 each, postage and packing free. I am under no obligation to purchase any books and may cancel my subscription at any time. The free books and gift will be mine to keep in any case.

N5ZED

Ms/Mrs/Miss/Mr ....Initials ....

Surname .... BLOCK CAPITALS PLEASE

Address ....

....

....Postcode...........................

Send this whole page to:
UK: FREEPOST CN81, Croydon, CR9 3WZ